Upstate Hustle

Upstate Hustle

Tasha Goins

www.urbanbooks.net

Urban Books, LLC
300 Farmingdale Road, N.Y.-Route 109
Farmingdale, NY 11735

ISBN 13: 978-1-64556-579-6
EBOOK ISBN: 978-1-64556-580-2

First Trade Paperback Printing May 2024
Printed in the United States of America

10 9 8 7 6 5 4 3 2 1

Distributed by Kensington Publishing Corp.
Submit Orders to:
Customer Service
400 Hahn Road
Westminster, MD 21157-4627
Phone: 1-800-733-3000
Fax: 1-800-659-2436

Dedicated to my beautiful mother, Carol Lee.

Mama, we made it.

Acknowledgments

Growing up in Upstate New York wasn't easy. We didn't have much, but I always had a big imagination. Once I picked up a book from my favorite writer, K'wan, he did something to me, giving me the vision that writing was a possibility. Author T. Styles, I appreciate you for giving me the understanding and game of the business side in the world of this book. Your hustle is impeccable. Lissha Sadler and Mrs. Toni Trina Franklin, I would like to express my deepest thanks and appreciation for making this possible.

Throughout this journey, I have learned that there was something special in me that I had never seen before, but I see it now. I have had to relieve so many traumas writing this book, but the healing and peace I have now are priceless.

Give me one reason why I can't, and I will show you five reasons to keep your good eye on my movement. I can guarantee you they're not ready for this *Upstate Hustle*.

Chapter 1

It was Saturday, and like clockwork, my mom and I visited her boyfriend, Jake, who was in prison. I was the only one that was forced to go to the visits; my brother David spent most of his time in the streets, and my brother Sammy spent his time on a football field. Both were rarely home during the day, so I had no choice but to go with her. Jake was currently serving a 15-year sentence, but I was always confused about how they met, since he was already in jail. My mom would just say they had mutual friends that hooked them up.

For two years, my mom dragged me back and forth with her on these visits. I hated coming to this place, especially on the weekends. I just wanted to chill with my friends, but I always ended up here with them, playing solitaire for eight straight hours. I felt the frustration weighing down on me while we were both searched by officers before the visit. After being searched, I was ready to go. The embarrassment I felt was never worth the time. But my mother didn't seem to mind. After her search, an officer always handed her a pink slip before we were allowed to walk into the gated area that leads into the prison.

We stood for a few moments, waiting for the door to open. My mother looked down at me and smiled before whispering, "Okay, Bella. We 'bout to go inside. You know what you have to do, right?"

"Yes, ma'am. I sit on the left side of the picnic table, directly in front of y'all, making sure I block the officer's view." I sighed heavily.

Ignoring my distress, she adjusted her short, flared red skirt and said, "Good job, babe."

The metal door behind us slammed closed, causing my stomach to start doing cartwheels as we waited for the gate to open. Once I heard the loud buzz alerting us that the front door of the prison was going to open, the thought of what was about to go down next made me sick.

There was another, shorter hallway we walked down that led us to the visiting area. As we walked in, all I could see were gray concrete walls wallpapered with rule posters and a small room to the left where they collected any care packages the families wanted to give the inmates. We continued to walk right past the bathrooms to the front desk that was in an open area looking out toward the inmates and their families.

The tables were square with metal chairs in rows placed in the center of the room, with multiple vending machines against the wall. The stench of cheap perfume mixed with funk invaded my nostrils. Covering my nose, I glanced up at mom as she handed her pink slip to the officer.

The officer grabbed the slip and picked up the phone. "Send inmate 16B0485 for a visit," he said as his voice vibrated through the room. Have a seat over there," he directed as he hung up the phone.

We found a place to sit as my mother pulled a full plastic bag of quarters out of her purse. "Here, Bella. Go and get you something to eat and drink," she said, handing me a handful of quarters out of the plastic bag.

"Okay," I said, holding out my hands as she placed the coins in my palms. Before I could finish filling my pockets, my mother gave me stern instructions.

"Bella, I'm going to get Jake's food. Come right back here and sit down when you're done until I get back," she said with narrowing eyes.

"Okay," I responded before I went on a journey to get enough snacks for what I thought I needed. After grabbing a soda, two candy bars, a few bags of chips, and a hard roll turkey sub, I went back to our table to wait for my mom.

I waited about a good thirty minutes before Mom would return. She would always get Jake the same thing every week: wings, a barbecued rib sandwich, a Twix, two bags of popcorn, and two sodas. After she placed the items on the table, she would cover them with a napkin until he came out.

"Ma, can I go and get a deck of cards?" I asked before she walked off again.

"Yeah, come right back because he should be out shortly, and we are going outside."

"Okay," I said, dreading the next few hours. Lowering my head in defeat, I walked back to the front desk with a deck of cards from the same officer who had checked us in. He was currently reading a magazine. "Excuse me, sir. May I have a pack of cards?"

Looking at me, he said, "Sure," as he reached over and pulled the cards out of the left drawer. "Make sure you bring them back before you leave," he ordered in a baritone voice as he handed me the cards.

"Okay," I replied before joining my mother back at the table as we continued to wait for him to come out.

About twenty minutes later, Jake walked out from behind a thick gray metal door into the family room. Jake stepped into the visitors' room looking like your average inmate. His long, black hair was cut in a mullet and slicked straight back into a ponytail. His skin had a tannish highlight due to the fact he was mixed with Indian,

German, and Black. Jake's state-issued greens were always creased to a tee, and his state-issued boots were always clean. He was looking fly under the circumstances. His pants had a makeshift hole in them, but I never saw it. I would hear my mom brag about the hole in his pants to her friend. It always stuck out to me as goofy.

We were sitting down until he got to the table. Rolling my eyes in annoyance, I got up and prepared to walk outside. I put the deck of cards and candy bars in my back pockets, one soda in each front pocket, and I carried the rest.

"Hey, babe, you look good," he said, smacking my mom on the ass.

"Thank you, babe." She smiled, leaning in for a kiss.

"Hey, Bella, You gettin' taller every time I see you," Jake said, gently rubbing the small of my back.

Putting on the fakest smile possible, I dryly spoke, "Hey, Jake. Thanks," as I wiggled a bit for him to move his hand. My mom and Jake picked up their food, and I followed them through the side door to the picnic area outside. Jake walked the yard like a superstar on the catwalk as he waved and nodded his head to everyone we passed. There was an officer sitting in a tall wooden chair with a ladder along the side that towered over the yard. Our eyes briefly made contact as we walked by. I waved and smiled. He nodded in response, then spoke to Jake.

"What's up, Jake."

"Same shit, different day, Jackson." He smiled as we continued to our table.

It was sunny outside as chatter from different people echoed around us. Once we got to the last picnic table on the left, I pulled everything out of my pockets and set them on the table before sitting down on the bench to eat. My mom and Jake sat down across from me and started nibbling too. Jake tried to make small talk with me before turning all his attention to my mom. Once I was finished with half of my snack, I straddled the bench, picking up the deck of cards, and I started playing solitaire to distract myself from their conversation.

After about thirty minutes, my mom let out a slight moan. *We ain't even been outside an hour yet,* I thought, lowering my head in embarrassment. I tried my hardest to focus on the cards and not watch, but it was unavoidable.

"Ahhh . . . Jake . . . mmm," she whispered in a low tone.

I looked over at the guard nervously, then back at my mom and Jake. I watched in disgust as she raised her hand to her mouth and casually spit in it, then placed her hand back underneath the table. Within minutes, Jake's face softened, and his eyes briefly stayed focused on me before rolling completely closed. All I could do was sit in silence, repeatedly flipping the cards over with an insincere smile on my face. Before long, I heard Jake let out a heavy sigh, then like magic, they were back to normal, talking about random things for the next few hours.

"Ma, can I go get another soda and use the bathroom?"

"Yes, hold on." she said before turning her attention back to Jake. "Babe, I'm about to take her to the bathroom and get her another soda. Do you want anything?" she asked him as we got up to go back inside the building.

"Naw, I'm good. Hurry yo' fine ass up." he replied before smacking the back of her thigh.

As we walked back, I said, "Ma, I'm ready to go. How much longer will we be here? It's hot, and I don't like the way he looks at me."

"Not much longer, and he ain't looking at no little girl when he has all of this grown woman," she said, turning up her nose.

I rolled my eyes and sucked my teeth, then walked in silence with her back to the main building. The bathroom was open, with one toilet, one sink, and metal box on the wall. A large black garbage can sat between the sink and a plastic changing table that hung off the wall. My mom placed her purse on the sink before lining the toilet with toilet paper. "Here, hurry up and use it, girl."

My stomach started to hurt as I sat down on the toilet seat. My mom was in the mirror, fixing her makeup and hair. Looking down, I noticed a red stain in my panties, and I started crying out.

"Ma . . . Ma, come here."

"What's wrong, Bella?" she said, looking at me through the mirror.

"Look, Ma," I said, pulling my pants down to my knees so she could see the blood in my underwear.

"You gotta be kidding me. Bella. Hold on," she barked, placing her lipstick back in her purse. She then grabbed her bag of quarters. Pulling out a quarter, she walked over to the metal box. Placing the quarter inside the slot, she then turned the metal lever clockwise, and a box slid out of the dispenser. She opened the box and pulled out the pad and placed it in my underwear, covering the blood.

"Wipe yourself good and come on and wash your hands."

"Okay," I said, wiping myself. I pulled my pants and underwear up, then flushed the toilet. Walking over to the sink, I washed and dried my hands while my mother used the bathroom. Wiping herself and fixing her clothes, she flushed the toilet and walked over to the sink to wash and dry her hands with a solid crease across her forehead. She was pissed, and I could tell.

"You have perfect timing," she said as we walked out of the bathroom. We headed back outside to the table in silence. Once we arrived, she gave Jake a look.

"What's wrong?" he asked with a look of concern.

"We gotta cut this short. Bella had an accident," she said with a look of defeat.

"Accident? What kind of an accident?" Jake asked, narrowing his eyes, confused.

"Female problems," she said, looking over at me.

"Ooooh, okay. I don't even know why you keep bringing her. Now our day is ruined," he said, cocking his head to the side.

"Jake, don't be that way. I will see you next Saturday," she said.

Stepping back, he said, "Take her home. I got other shit I can do inside," before walking off.

I looked at my mom. She was holding back the tears as she gathered the trash on the table. "Bella, help me clear this table so we can go."

"Yes, ma'am," I replied, doing as I was told. Once the table was clear, I looked to my mother and said, "I'm sorry to ruin your day."

"It's not your fault," she said, wiping the tears from each cheek. "Let's go."

When we arrived home, we pulled into the driveway. Before getting out of the car, my mother said, "Go take a bath and change your clothes when we get in this house, Bella. I'm about to change and go to the bar."

"Yes, ma'am," I replied as we got out of the car and headed to the back door. I hated how the apartment was covered in old, dark green shingles. It was ugly, but big inside. We stayed downstairs, and my mom's best friend, Mary, stayed upstairs. She and her husband owned the house, and we moved in about three years ago, right before he got arrested for his second DUI. Mary and my mom became close friends after that.

As I walked in the back door of the dimly lit apartment, the smell of stale cigarettes with a faint stench of booze amongst the funk impacted my nose. My brother's bedroom was to the right just before we entered the kitchen. The only light that could be seen came from the television in the distance, which sat on a big black stand in front of the living room window. Walking ahead of me, my mother turned on the kitchen light, placing her purse on the counter before heading to her room. "Oh, and Bella, don't forget to wash your underwear and hang them up when you're done."

"Yes, ma'am," I replied.

"Your brothers should be home soon. Make yourself a sandwich till then," she said, walking into her bedroom.

Our house was spacious for a two-bedroom on the north side of the city, but there was always a messy clutter somewhere. My brother's room door was open. I could smell their stank-ass socks. I hurried up trying to close the door, but their trash and clothes stopped me. Glancing in, I shook my head. As I turned around, I walked through the kitchen into the dining room. Last week's laundry was still piled on our wooden dining room table.

The dining room was large enough that my mom divided it into two sides with a brown wicker divider. My daybed sat on the far left side near the window, with my clothes and toys scattered on the bed and floor. At the end of my bed sat a closet, which was used as storage, and across from that was the bathroom we all shared. Not more than five steps outside of my room sat the living room and then the front door. Across from that was my mother's room, which had a door that connected her room to the bathroom.

Walking over to turn off the TV, I froze as breaking news flashed across the screen. The white lady's next set of words blew my mind.

"Breaking news: There has been a murder-suicide in Niagara Falls." I stood as the news anchor continued to speak. "This evening, fifty-year-old Willie Goins is dead—"

Once I heard the name Willie Goins, my heart dropped. I turned up the television, while calling my mother to the living room. "Ma . . . come look at the TV!" I yelled, bracing myself for her reaction to the news of his death.

I had just seen him briefly last week, for the first time in years. I walked into the house from my friend's birthday party, and there he was, sitting on the couch and talking to my mother like he'd never left. I had no clue he even knew where we lived. He was in bad shape and looked nothing like the coward that had boldly left his family behind so many years ago for some pussy. The memories I had of him were not great. My parents argued and fought all the time. My dad ended up leaving my mom when I was six years old for Tracey, my babysitter.

My mom was a nervous wreck after that. She started drinking heavily and using drugs regularly. My dad barely came back around the family, rarely called, and never sent money. For me, the man I knew as my father died the day he left us.

There was no love lost for him from me, but I sympathized with the fact that my mother and brothers would not take this news well. They had experienced him as a loving father. I never got that experience nor connection with him.

A few minutes later, my mom came into the living room. "What?" she yelled, turning on the light. "Bella, do you hear me? What?"

"Look," I said, pointing to the TV screen as the rest of the news anchor's words echoed through the room.

"After fatally shooting his ex-girlfriend, thirty-year-old Tracey Williams, Goins turned the gun on himself. We don't have any further information at this time," she said before cutting to the next story.

"Oh my God," she cried as tears started to roll down her cheeks at the devastating news. A flood of emotions came over me, not for him, but for my mother's pain. For me, all the years of unanswered questions would forever remain unanswered by a man who never acknowledged me as his. A man that missed every birthday, every skinned knee, and anything else I ever did. I couldn't understand how she had so much sadness for a man that left her and her kids for dead.

The news of his death spread like wildfire around the city. About a week later, friends and family came together in a homegoing ceremony to celebrate his life. I was shocked to see so many people in attendance. As much as I felt like I should cry, my emotions wouldn't allow me to shed a tear for a man who was never around.

After his funeral, life went back to normal. It was now Friday, and I was getting dressed to go outside when the phone rang. Jumping off my bed, I ran to the kitchen to answer it.

"Hello."

"Bella, we are going to visit Jake in the morning, so don't be out playing too late," Momma said.

"Okayy." I sighed, rolling my eyes. "Ma, can I go with Sammy to the field? I don't want to go this Saturday." It was bad enough that school was getting ready to start in a few weeks. I had the worst summer vacation ever because every Saturday I was stuck in that place with them.

"I will think about it, girl. And tell David to make you guys some grits and eggs. Where is Sammy?"

"Sammy went to practice, and David ain't here."

"Where is David?" she asked, sucking her teeth.

"I don't know. David ain't never here like that no more," I replied, holding the phone to my ear with my shoulder as I twisted my fingers in the phone cord.

Sighing heavily into the phone, she said, "I swear . . . Okay, make you a bowl of cereal or something till later. And tell his ass to call me when he gets home, 'cause he ain't grown. He just don't come and go as he pleases. Always in them gotdamn streets," she ranted.

"Yes, ma'am."

"Let me get back to work."

"Yes, ma'am. Have a good day," I said with no reply from her, just a dial tone.

I hung up the phone and went to make myself a bowl of cereal, but we had no milk left. I looked all around for something to eat and found one packet of instant oatmeal in the cabinet. I made a bowl of oatmeal and sat on the couch to eat and watch cartoons. When I was done, I placed the bowl on the table and headed outside to play.

I played outside in Kayla's yard until I saw the streetlights come on. "Kayla, I gotta hurry home," I said as I took off running down the street to my house. Just as I got to the driveway, my mom was pulling in. *Oh, man. I made it just in time*, I thought, waiting for her to get out of the car.

Once she stepped out of the car, I yelled, "Hey, Ma."

"Hey. Are your brothers home yet?" she asked, closing the car door.

"I don't know. I've been at Kayla's house all day," I replied as we headed in the house.

Once inside, my mom kicked off her shoes and put her purse on the counter. "I'm about to order you a pizza before I go to the bar."

"Yes, ma'am," I said, grabbing my bowl off the coffee table.

Moments later, Sammy came busting in the house.

"Ma! Ma!"

"What!"

"I heard David got arrested last night on Washburn and Lewis. He was hanging wit' Wes and dem when the cops ran up in the trap. They got raided, Ma."

"What? I told his ass to stay off the muthafuckin' block wit' dem niggas. How you find out?"

"Low told me at practice. His brother got arrested too."

"Shit. I ain't bailing his ass out either, 'cause that's what he gets. Let me call the police station and see where they are holding him," she said, picking up the phone.

My world was shattered. Who was going to look out for me? Sammy was always at practice, and even though David stayed in the streets, he still made sure I was straight before he left, because most days, my mom was at the bar when she got off work. My nerves were bad just thinking about it.

The next day, we went to visit Jake, but this visit was a little different. My mom was making calls until late in the night, trying to find out where David was being held.

As we made our way down the hall, I was shocked she gave me no pep talk. When we got to the visiting area, there was a bit of a line. While in line, I asked my mom if I could get a deck of cards, but the answer was no. Once we got in the visiting area and grabbed snacks, Jake came through the doors.

"Hey, babe, you look good," he said, smacking my mom on the ass.

"Thank you, babe," she said dryly as tears formed in her eyes.

"Hey, Bella—"

"Wuz going on, babe?" he asked with a look of concern on his face.

"David got picked up by the Feds."

"Damn, let's head outside to the picnic table so you can tell me everything," Jake said, grabbing my mother's hand.

"Thank you, babe. Come on, Bella," she said quickly as Jake guided her outside to the picnic table with me hot on their heels.

I wanted to hear their conversation, so I tried my best to keep up behind them. *Who is he to talk about my brother anyway? We haven't had a man in the house since my father left, and we don't need one now, especially him.* My thoughts were going a mile a minute. I needed as much information as possible so I could let Sammy know what was going on. Once we got to the table and sat down, my mom instantly started crying. I said nothing, just listened and watched.

"When this happen? Does he have a bail yet?" Jake questioned.

"Last night. No, not yet. The Feds ain't givin' out any information."

"Shit, he will be all right then. Do you know if he got caught with anything?"

"I really don't know any details yet. Sammy came home after practice and told me. When I get back to the house, I will try calling around and see what information I can get to piece this shit together."

"Baby, breathe. This is what I was talking about. Them niggas need a man in the household. I know you been holding it down, but you need me there to help you regulate they ass. Look, I'm gon' need you to go home and look up federal lawyers. They will be your best bet at this point. I only have about another year up in here, and then I will be there to help you."

I wanted to get a better understanding of what he meant by saying we needed a man like him in the house.

Is she really going to let him live with us? Even after I told her he made me uncomfortable?

"Okay! You are so good to me. This is some bullshit," she said, slamming her hands on the table. "I can't catch a break, Jake. I know you will be home, but that is a whole year. What am I supposed to do till then?" she asked with tears in her eyes, getting up from the table.

"Come on, Bella."

"Yes, ma'am," I said as both Jake and I stood up simultaneously, looking at her, confused. We could tell how frustrated she was, but what could either of us do?

"This ain't the place to lose your cool. Don't shut me out," Jake said in a calming voice.

"You're right, babe." Reaching out for a hug, she whispered, "I'm sorry. I just don't know what to do."

"I told you the other night what needed to be done, but we gon' get through all this shit. I gotchu," he said, releasing their embrace. "Head home and call that lawyer. I will give you a call in the morning."

"Okay, babe. Let's go, Bella."

"Yes, ma'am," I said, feeling like I was in an episode of the *Twilight Zone.*

Within the next two weeks, Jake and my mother were married in a jailhouse wedding. She didn't even bother to tell me and Sammy until after they were married. First our dad died, then David got arrested, and now this. The whole situation was making my nerves bad.

Chapter 2

One Year Later

The day was here for Jake to be released from prison. He moved right in with us the same day he was released. It was like something switched on in my mother the day before he came home, turning her into Betty Crocker. My mother started cooking and cleaning the house from top to bottom, demanding that Sam and I assisted her.

"Bella, Sammy, hurry up cleaning those rooms," she said, banging pots and pans in the kitchen. With no response from either of us, she yelled, "Sammy! Bella! Do y'all hear me talking to you?"

"Yes, ma'am. I'm done. Just getting ready to take a shower and get dressed. When will the food be ready?"

"Dressed? To go where? And this food is not for y'all. It's for Jake when he comes home tomorrow. I will order a pizza for y'all before I go to the bar," she said, now standing in the dining room with her hands on her hips.

"To go outside and play," I replied, confused. "Wait, we can't eat the food till tomorrow?" I said, screwing up my face as confusion painted a solid frown. Just then, Sammy stepped out of his room at ten.

"This was too much. Jake's moving in, while David is still locked up. Now you finally cook in who knows how long, and we can't eat it because it's for dat nigga. Ma, you are more worried about Jake than the rest of us,"

Sammy yelled, throwing his hands in the air, revealing his anger as he walked out of the house, slamming the door behind him.

"Sam!" she yelled right before the door slammed. "Bella, you're not going outside until you clean the living room, vacuum, and clean the bathroom," she demanded, sucking her teeth and walking back into the kitchen.

"What? But why?" I asked as my blood began to boil. Why all of a sudden was she into the house being cleaned, and on top of that, demanding me and Sammy clean up too, just because Jake was coming here?

"Bella, don't start with me. Do as I said, li'l girl," she yelled as she walked in her room, slamming the door behind her.

"Uggh!" I yelled, sucking my teeth. "This is so unfair," I complained, starting the list of chores I had been given before getting dressed to go outside. *This wouldn't be happening if David was here.* I thought about picking up the living room first. Jake moving in was the start of our family changing and divided forever. My mother was changing into someone that I had never seen before, and for what? Jake?

By the time I cleaned up and got dressed, everyone was gone. My mom left money on the counter with a note that read, *Sam, order the pizza.* I put the note and money back on the counter and headed outside to play.

Like clockwork, when the streetlights came on, I was in the house, but my mom and Sammy were still not home. I hopped in the shower and put my pajamas on. After picking up the bathroom, I plopped down on the couch and turned on the TV. Before I knew it, Sammy was waking me up because I had fallen asleep.

"Bella, did you eat?" He was smelling like he bathed in a bottle of Jack.

"No. Momma left money for you to order pizza," I said, rubbing my eyes. "What's that smell? Have you been drinking, Sammy?" I said, holding my nose.

"Figures. I got you some Micky D's. It's on the dining room table. Knowing her, she is probably still at the bar," he said before walking in his room.

Jumping up off the couch, I ran in the dining room and grabbed the bag off the table. Shoving my hand in the bag, I pulled out a handful of fries then shoved them in my mouth as I sat down. Moments later, Sammy opened his door. I heard him open the cabinet then the fridge. I was swinging my feet back and forth, enjoying my meal when I heard the sound of foil. At that moment, I froze and yelled, "Sammy!" Jumping up from the table, I ran into the kitchen. "Sammy, no!" I yelled. "Momma said—"

"Fuck what Momma said," Sammy spat, dipping his spoon into the dish that was meant for Jake.

"Oohhhhh."

"Shut up. Let me worry about Momma. Now, clean up and go to bed, Bella," Sammy said, placing his food in the microwave.

I couldn't believe it. Sammy was declaring war. He, of all people, was getting ready to go head up with Momma. Shaking my head, I cleaned up my mess and headed to bed. *I'm gonna need Dave to come home soon*, I thought, turning off my light and getting in bed.

The next morning, my mom woke me up early. "Bella, get up and straighten the house. I'm going to pick up Jake."

"Yes, ma'am," I said as I stretched and rubbed my eyes.

"Me and Jake will be home around noon, and I want the house cleaned up," she said, leaving out the door.

I got up and grabbed some cereal before getting dressed. Sammy still hadn't come out of his room. Lightly tapping on his bedroom door, I watched as it slowly creaked open. Sammy was not even home, and his bed hadn't been slept in. *Where is he at?* I thought, walking over to the kitchen. I climbed on top of the counter, opening one cabinet. I grabbed my favorite bowl and placed it on the counter. Opening another cabinet, I grabbed the box of Lucky Charms and placed it on the counter. Jumping down off the counter, I turned to open the fridge when I noticed a note with my name on it from my mom. She had left me a whole list of things for me to clean up before going outside.

"Ugh. She is doing the most. Like, why would he care if the house was clean or dirty? He is coming from jail," I mumbled, sucking my teeth. I opened the fridge door and grabbed the milk. Walking over to the counter, I set it down next to the open box of Lucky Charms and the bowl before I grabbed my spoon. As I fixed my bowl of cereal, the phone rang.

"Hello," I said, shoveling a spoonful of cereal in my mouth.

"Bella, is Mom home?"

With my mouth full, I replied, "Nope," chewing the rest of my cereal before clearing my throat. "David?"

"Yeah, sis. Where is she at? I need to talk to her," he said in a frustrated tone.

"When will you be home?" I asked, talking between spoonfuls. "So much has been going on since you left, Dave," I said, trying to hurry up and chew before I started filling him in on everything that had happened.

"Word! Damn. Soon, sis."

"Yup. She was tripping right along with Sammy's ass. What's soo–" Before I could finish my sentence, David cut me off.

"Watch ya mouth!" he hissed. "That nigga only moving in 'cause I'm not there, but I will be soon. Aye, tell Sammy to keep his cool. Tell Momma I'm gonna call her later. I gotta go. Love ya."

"Love you too, David."

Hanging up the phone, I looked down at an almost empty bowl. Taking my last two bites, I put the bowl in the sink and headed outside.

After playing outside for a few hours, I saw Sammy coming up the block.

"Sammy," I said as I took off running to tell him about the call from David, and making sure I gave him the message. He didn't really respond, just kind of grunted as he continued to walk. I followed behind him as we headed to the house.

When we walked in the house, the sounds echoed through the house from my mom's room. "Awww, Jake. Mmm." She moaned louder and louder.

Covering my ears, I yelled, "They doing that nasty stuff?"

Sammy pulled my hands down and said, "Go back outside and be in when the streetlights come on."

"Okay," I said, turning around and going back outside.

I couldn't believe what my mom and Jake were doing. Just the thought made me nauseous. *Eww, she's nasty,* I thought, closing the door behind me as I took off running back to Kayla's house. Kayla was my best friend since third grade. We shared everything, and I was certainly sharing this.

Once at her house, I pulled the green screen door open and knocked on the door, but there was no response. "Kayla, Kayla," I yelled, knocking just a little bit harder before shutting the screen door and skipping down the street back to my house.

Once in my driveway, I heard Momma screaming and cursing in the house. Running full speed up the driveway, I ran up the back stairs, skipping two of the four steps. I busted through the back door so I would not miss my front row seat to the drama that was unfolding. World War III was happening right now in my kitchen between Momma and Sammy.

"Sammy, what the fuck is your problem?" she yelled, holding the pan of mac and cheese that she told us not to touch.

"Ma, you trippin'. What the fuck? Calm down. You're making a big deal over me eating some mac and cheese?" Sammy said, waving her off as he headed to the living room.

"Didn't I say this was Jake's dinner and not to eat it?" she yelled, slamming the pan of mac cheese on the dining room table, her face redder than a pickled beet.

Walking up behind my mom, I could see the inside of the pan once it hit the table. Man, the pan was empty from the left corner of the pan to the center. "Oooooooohhh," I taunted Sammy as I followed behind Momma, who was now right on the back of his heels. "Ma, I told him. See, Sammy, what I say? But nobody listens to me," I instigated.

It was about to go down when my mom paused mid step and without turning around, raised her hand and yelled, "Bella, take yo' ass in that bathroom and wash your muthafuckin' hands so you can get ready for dinner."

"Ugh. Yes, ma'am," I said, turning on the bathroom light and the faucet so my mom wouldn't notice my head sticking out of the bathroom. "I'm not missing this," I mumbled. At that moment, I saw Jake come out of the room, throwing on a shirt. He almost bumped into Momma.

Holding up his hands to stop her, he said, "What's wrong, babe? Is everything okay?"

"No. Sammy got into the food. I made it for us." She broke down in tears.

"Breathe, baby," he said, raising his hands to Momma's face before kissing her forehead. "We have plenty more dinners to eat together. It's okay," he said, brushing her hair down on both sides.

"Jake, you're absolutely right," she said as her red face faded back to her natural pale complexion.

Jake then turned his attention to Sammy, who was standing at the front door. Just as he was about to open the door and walk out, Jake said, "Sammy, man, it's cool. You ain't gotta go nowhere. Let's just sit down, chill, and get to know each other. Aye, I hear you play football. The Buffalo Bills vs. Jets game is getting ready to come on," he said as he plopped down on the couch and grabbed the remote.

Sammy hesitated, then gave in, walking over and plopping down on the other end of the couch next to him.

"Say, babe, can you warm the food up and we all sit in the living room instead tonight? Oh, and bring us both a glass of Kool Aid."

"Sure, babe," she said, walking past the bathroom, cutting her eyes at me. "Hurry up, miss thang. I need your help."

"Yes, ma'am." Stepping back in the bathroom, I washed my hands then turned off the faucet. Exiting the bathroom, I paused, looking at Sammy getting real comfortable with Jake. "I know David ain't gonna like this," I mumbled as I went to help Momma in the kitchen.

As I walked in the kitchen, the phone rang.

"I got it," she said. "Hey, babe, how are you holding up?"

"Ma," I said, standing next to her. "Is that David?"

"What?" she said, placing one hand over the receiver.

"Is that David?" I whispered.

"Yes. Now, get my good plates and place them by the stove, Bella," she said, waving me off as she continued her conversation.

"What the fuck is wrong with you?" she said as a crease formed across her forehead. She placed one hand on her hip. "Ah huh . . . When is your court date?" she asked, grabbing a pen and piece of paper while she continued to talk. "Okay, I love you. Okay, we 'bout to eat, but I will be there. Look, don't start! Okay, see you tomorrow," she said before hanging up the phone.

I climbed up on the counter, opened the cabinet, and pulled down the good plates. *She is doing too much. Paper plates will be fine for him. She is acting like he is something special.*

"Babe, is the food almost ready?" Jake yelled from the couch. "Who was that on the phone?"

"That was David on the phone, and dinner is coming right up, babe," she said, fixing Jake's plate, then placing it in the microwave. Once his food was warmed up, she called Sammy to get the drinks for everyone.

"Bella, go give it to Jake. Be careful. It's hot."

Carefully grabbing the plate, I walked into the living room. "Here ya go," I said, handing the plate to Jake.

"Thanks, kiddo," he said, reaching his hand out and grabbing the plate as he brushed his fingers across mine, smiling and giving me a wink.

I quickly walked back into the kitchen as Momma heated up the rest of the plates. My mouth watered as the delicious aroma of mac and cheese and fried chicken filled the air. I was hungry, and my stomach started to growl. My mom rarely cooked like this. Normally, we just ordered a pizza, and she went to the bar.

We all found seats in the living room. This time, Momma was sitting next to Jake, and Sammy was sitting in the love seat.

"This is good, baby," Jake said, rubbing her hand.

"Yeah, Ma, it is," Sammy agreed, licking his lips together.

"Momma, this is really good," I said before taking a bite of my cornbread.

"Thank you." She smiled and started to eat.

"Ma, what David says?" I asked, readjusting myself on the floor.

"What? David called? I miss him again? Why didn't anybody say anything?" Sammy whined.

"It wasn't even like that. Chill the fuck out. He couldn't talk long, Sammy."

"When is the court date?" Jake asked, taking a bite of his chicken.

"It's this Monday, I think," she said, taking a bite of her cornbread.

"I can't go. I gotta go see about that construction gig. What did the attorney say?"

"He will call me tomorrow. But when I hired him, he said he could get David home. Mr. Jackson got it."

"Bitch should've had my brother home first," Sammy mumbled under his breath, clearly upset, shaking his head back and forth as he continued to eat, thinking nobody heard what he said.

"Whoa, whoa, whoa, who are you talking to? Is there a problem, boy?" Jake said with bass in his voice. Leaning in, he pounded his fist on the table. "Look, I understand, this last year has been hard. Your father just passed, your brother is locked up, and now I'm here."

"You don't know shit," Sammy said, throwing his plate on the floor. "Matter of fact, don't speak on my father or my brother," Sammy barked, crossing his arms aggressively, his eyes starting to water.

"I ain't trying to replace y'all father or y'all brother," Jake said, pausing for a moment, giving Sammy and me a death stare.

"This whole situation is bullshit, Ma. You should have gotten David out. How could you just leave your son in jail like this? Now you just gonna let this nigga come in here and take over."

"Who are you talking to?" Getting up from her seat, she was pointing her finger at him. "You disrespectful motherfucker, I pay these bills around here," she yelled.

Before Ma could move or Sammy could utter another word, Jake bum rushed toward Sammy, pushing him in his chest. Sammy swung and missed. Jake scooped up Sammy, slamming him to the ground. They started tussling on the floor, rolling back and forth, throwing punches at each other.

My eyes widened as everything unfolded. Sammy had a point about how she brought Jake home before David. The better question was, why would she bring him home first because he just got in the family? Faintly turning my head to Sammy, I saw his brass eyes lock in on me. I looked over at my mother to defend Sammy. She was looking at Jake with pride in her eyes. *Is she choosing him over us?* I thought before screaming, "Stop it! Stop it!" My eyes widened as everything unfolded. "Get off my brother. Ma, do something," I said, getting up to try to help Sammy. Breathing heavily, my heart rate increasing, I shook as I was balling up my little fists.

Looking around, the first thing I saw was the glass pitcher that was partially full of Kool Aid on the table. Instantly raising my arm behind my head without a thought, I swung the pitcher. *Crack!* It connected perfectly on the back of Jake's head.

Disoriented, Jake stood up, stumbling just a little. "You bitch," he spat.

"Jake, babe . . . Nooo!" Momma yelled, grabbing his arm before he could backhand me.

Snatching his arm away from her, he spat, "Let me go," as he scanned the room, staring death into our souls.

Jake grabbed the back of his head, touching the minor wound.

"The bottom line is y'all will respect *us*. That's what the fuck I do know, regardless if you like it or not," he said, making sure his authority was felt. "Y'all kids have been out of control. Got yo' momma worrying and upset every day. Well, I'm here now, and the shit gon' stop. Now, clean up that mess, li'l nigga."

Backing up, my mother gave him her full attention. "Babe, I understand, but you gotta understand they have been through a lot." She cried, looking over at me and Sammy. Turning her fury to me, she screamed, "Bella, what the fuck is wrong with you? You need to stay in a child's place, because you could have gotten hurt."

"Babe. Babe," he interrupted, pacing back and forth, shaking his head. "I'm sorry. I know you worked hard to make this day special for me. I know things got out of hand. I'm so sorry. I just couldn't sit and let the disrespect continue," he said, looking over at her, seeking her forgiveness before walking into the bathroom and slamming the door behind him.

"I hate you. You let this nigga come in here and beat my ass like this his house," Sammy said, getting up from the floor and adjusting his clothes. "Fuck this shit," he spat before walking out of the front door.

"Bella, don't think you got away with shit," she hissed. "Clean up this mess," she said, cocking her head to the side. She gave me the ultimate stare of death before she turned on her heels to see about Jake.

"Yes, ma'am," I replied softly, my eyes filled with tears. I couldn't believe that I was trying to help Sammy, because clearly, she wasn't going to help him. She just watched as Jake beat Sammy's ass in our house. That was a violation. He was just a guest.

I watched Momma knock on the bathroom door frantically. "Baby, baby, open the door," she cried hysterically before it slowly opened, and she walked in, closing the door behind her.

Sitting down on the edge of the couch, I began to cry as I ran back everything that had just happened. *Lord, what kind of man has she let in our family?* I thought, burying my face deep into my palms. all I could do was weep at the thought of what life would be now that he was living here.

Chapter 3

One Year Later

Sammy and I were excited that David was finally coming home. Momma went to pick him up alone because Jake was working. We liked that it would just be us without any outsiders. While we waited, I pulled out my markers, crayons, and craft paper to make him a welcome home poster, and Sammy cleaned up the bedroom.

When Mom and David arrived, both Sammy and I were in the kitchen, yelling, "Welcome home!"

Walking in the house, David's eyes lit up. "Yooo! Awww, man. I missed y'all."

My mom walked in after him, placing her purse and keys on the counter. "Okay, I gotta get back to work. Y'all order something," she said, opening her purse. Momma pulled a twenty-dollar bill out and placed it on the counter before heading in the bathroom.

David smiled. "I see Ma hasn't changed."

We all let out a laugh that echoed through the kitchen. Moments later, she stepped out of the bathroom, grabbing her purse and keys. "Okay, Jake and I are going to the casino after we get off. Whatever y'all do, make sure my house stays clean," she ordered before she walked out the door.

After David got situated, we all piled on the couch. Sammy ordered us pizza, while David found a movie for us to watch. Once the pizza was delivered, we sat around and chilled like the old days, filling David in on all that had been going on. He sat intensely as we talked, not saying much between bites.

"Bro, what are we gon to do?" Sammy asked, taking another bite.

Not missing a beat, my eye flashed between the two of them as I stuffed my face with pizza, waiting for a reaction. David leaned back into the couch, looking out the window with no reply.

"You ain't gonna say shit?" Sammy snapped, confused by David's silence.

"First off, Sammy, you were in the wrong, yo," he said, wiping his mouth. David placed his plate on the table. "At no time should disrespecting Momma be an option. That nigga being her husband, he was supposed to check you for that."

"What the fuck? Oh, so you taking dis nigga side over your brother. What the fuck? This some birds of a feather type shit you got going on, my nigga," he said, throwing his napkin and plate down as he stood up.

I choked while taking a sip of my soda from my head moving so fast as I looked at the confusion in front of me. I couldn't believe our family gathering got this heated and we all had just got back together. Before I knew it, David was off the couch and in Sammy's face. They stood nose to nose in the middle of the living room, preparing to fight.

"Wait. Hold on. What y'all doin'?" I shouted out, jumping up to separate them and dropping my Sprite and plate on the floor. Posting myself in the small space between them, I spread my arms wide, trying to put distance between these two giants. As their bodies tossed me from side to side, I yelled, "It's 'posed to be us against the world, remember?"

"Move the fuck out the way, Bella," David said, pushing me to the couch like a rag doll. He stepped back, glaring at Sammy with fire in his eyes. "Nigga, right is right and wrong is wrong, bro. You was outta line my nigga. Dat nigga could never replace Dad, and on some real shit, Dad was never really here in the first place. But this, my nigga, is Ma house," David said, pointing to the wall. "She deserves respect and to be happy, right? We gon' see how dis shit plays out, Sam," David reasoned. "I was gone for a minute, and in that time, I experienced a lot, and I saw a lot. I fucked myself outta freedom with my own choice. Do I regret them? No. But I acknowledge that I fucked up," he said, pointing to his chest.

"That's not the point." Sammy interrupted, throwing his hands up. "She brought this nigga in off the streets, straight outta jail. What the fuck type shit is that?"

"Sammy, David does have a point. This is Ma hou—" Before I could get my sentence out, they both looked over at me and yelled.

"Shut up! Ain't nobody talking to you, Bella."

Smacking my lips, I rolled my eyes and began gathering plates and soda cans. "All I know is if y'all tear up Momma house, we all gettin' a beat down, but y'all niggas will both be homeless," I spat before walking in the kitchen. "Which one of y'all cleaning that rug up?" I yelled as I placed everything in the trash, grabbing another garbage bag from the cabinet. "Y'all niggas making my nerves bad," I yelled, snatching my robe off my bed and walking in the bathroom to hop in the shower. It was time to get ready for school the next day, and this whole situation had my head spinning.

These two are really about to fight in Momma's living room over a dumb disagreement, I thought, getting in the shower. I was drained and ready to lay my head down. It was just like ole times. The peace between us never lasted long.

***

After about a month, I saw less and less of David, but when he did come, I always got a new pair of sneakers or a fresh fit from him. For the first time, my brother had a job that brought in real money. David never really had money, so now that he was making some, I was glad to be the proud recipient. Most of the time, I would be the only one home after school. I would make myself a sandwich until my mom got home. Most days, he would leave money and a note on the counter for me to order myself a pizza after school.

Sammy seemed to be all over the place. He had stopped playing football and was cutting school more to hang with his friends. The school year was almost over. Why would he wait until now to mess up? I had no clue.

Now that Jake was working in the roofing business and doing construction on the side, things turned around for us. They got me a new bed with matching dressers, there was new furniture in the living room, and we never ran out of food to eat.

One day, while watching TV, I heard them talking in the kitchen.

"Babe, Bella needs her own room. We need to let her get the boys' room since them niggas ain't never home," Jake suggested.

"Bella is just fine where she is. Sammy and David need their own space, because they are growing into men. Don't nobody wanna see they asses running around here half naked," Momma protested.

"I understand that, but she needs her own too. Let's go in the room. I got something to run by you," Jake said, walking out of the kitchen with Momma in tow.

The summer was upon us. Jake and Momma would be gone almost every weekend. It wasn't long before he and my brothers started bumping heads again, which meant a lot of tension in the house, especially with him and David. He expected them to be home with me if he and Momma had plans, so I wouldn't be alone. Sometimes, I would get to stay with Kayla and her family, but most weekends when they were gone, I would be the only one home. But I didn't mind. I kind of enjoyed having the house to myself. I was able to watch TV and eat what I wanted, never needing to clean up right away. I felt like an adult. Of course, my mom's homegirl upstairs would check on me from time to time, but for the most part, I was the boss.

It was the last week of school, and report cards were sent home. After school, I ran to the bus, excited because I'd made all As and Bs. I couldn't wait to get home and tell Momma when she called to check in. When I got off the bus and started heading home, I noticed Momma's car was in the driveway. When I walked in, Momma was on the phone, a serious look on her face. So, I just placed my report card on the counter and went to change my clothes.

I wonder what that call is about, I thought, plopping down on the couch to watch some TV.

About an hour later, Sammy walked in the door, and all hell broke loose. I peeped my head over to look on as the fireworks unfolded.

Momma started cursing and fussing like it was World War III. "Nigga, where the fuck you been? I just got off the phone with your counselor, Sammy, and she told me yo' ass failed three classes and needed to go to summer school. What the fuck is wrong with you?" she yelled, cursing Sammy all the way out.

I got off the couch and ran to the kitchen to taunt my older brother. "Ohhhhh, Sammy, you failed three classes," I interjected.

"Bella, mind yo business. Matter of fact, take yo' ass outside," Momma yelled. "Sammy, I'm not done with you. Sit yo' ass down," she ordered, pointing her finger to the living room.

I took my time going outside because I knew Sammy was in big trouble and I didn't want to miss the action. I could feel my mother's stares. Looking back, I locked eyes with my mom, and that was all I needed to see to make me hurry up outside. I was not trying to be next on her ass-whoopin' list, so I headed to Kayla's house.

Later that night at dinner, everyone at the table was quiet. There was so much tension in the air that I was afraid to breathe too heavily. Momma cleared her voice and made an announcement that sent me and Sammy over the edge, but David seemed to remain quiet. "Jake and I have been talking, and we think it best for us to move. He has a good job opportunity in Baker that is more money and will put us in a good position. We are all piled on top of each other in this house, and everyone needs more space," she said before taking a sip of her water.

"What?" Sammy and I both yelled in unison.

"Listen, kids, this job opportunity is good, and Sammy, it will allow you to get back on track in school," Jake added.

"This dat bullshit!" Sammy spat, getting up from the table and going right to his room.

"Ma, I won't have any friends. What am I supposed to do? This is not fair," I cried, distraught by the current decision that was being made. But what could I do about it?

David didn't say a word. He just got up from the table and walked out the door.

Chapter 4

Within a month, we were packed and moved to the dull town of Baker. All I saw was pure country for miles when we pulled up to the house. Me and my brothers looked at each other and frowned at our new neighborhood. It was nothing like Lockport. Everything was so far apart and plain. We all poured out of the car, looking over at my mom, who was kissing Jake's face multiple times. With stars in her eyes as she headed to the house, she smiled and said, "I love it, Jake. This house is so big. Okay, y'all, grab the stuff out the car while Jake and I open the door."

We looked at each other before unloading the items we had packed up in the car.

"Dis dat bullshit," Sammy mumbled.

"Shut up, nigga. Let's get this shit over wit'. I got someplace to be," David spat, grabbing a box.

"Where you goin', David? Back to Lockport? I wanna go." I started grabbing my suitcase.

"No," he replied in the driest tone.

This new town brought a mix of emotions for me. Saying goodbye to my friends, especially Kayla, was my biggest challenge at the age of fifteen. With Baker being a small town, there were only a hundred or so families residing within a two-mile radius. It was nothing like living in Lockport.

All the kids attended the same school but in different buildings. I was able to go to school with Sammy, which offered a sense of reassurance in the midst of change.

Our new caramel-colored house stood in the middle
of East Ave. The house had one large bedroom and bathroom downstairs. It was definitely bigger. We even had
a garage that was attached to the right side of the house,
which I envisioned as my clubhouse. There was also a
finished basement that my brothers instantly claimed as
their party spot. The other three bedrooms were upstairs.
Up the stairs to the right was a room with my name on
the door, a bathroom to the left, and then two more
rooms down a short hall, one room on each side.

When I walked into my room, that's when I saw my
new best friend. Momma and Jake got me a dog.

"Oh my God!" I yelled.

Moments later, Mom and Jake walked in behind me.
"Surprise!" she shouted.

"Just for you, baby girl. What will you name him?" Jake
smiled.

"Buddy," I said.

After being in Baker for three months, I found there
was one other black family in town that Momma and
I met at the grocery store. The kids seemed a little off,
nothing like my friends back in Lockport. Most of the
neighbors around us were mostly old and white. I don't
see myself making any friends in this place. Most of
the time, I watched TV and played with my dog to keep
myself company if I wasn't in the basement with my
brothers.

I walked downstairs to grab a bag of chips out of
the kitchen. The house reflected Momma's minimal
decorating skills. Whatever she found was what was put
in the house. In the backyard, Jake had set up a swing
and added a small garden on the left side of the house, a
hobby that puzzled us all. I can't even tell you what he

was growing because it all looked like a bunch of bushes to me. I never saw many fruits or veggies growing over there.

Momma didn't want Buddy in the house, so Jake built him a doghouse in the back yard. Summer break was almost over, and school was getting ready to start in a few weeks. It was the middle of the week, and Momma promised we would go school shopping today. After taking my shower and getting dressed, I started doing my chores. It was just me and Momma today, Jake was gone to work, and one of David's friends came to pick him and Sammy up earlier.

After I cleaned my room and bathroom, I headed downstairs to vacuum and clean the living room, when I heard Momma on the phone fussin'. "What the hell? Girl, oh hell naw," Momma said, slamming something down on the counter.

I wondered who she was talking to, so I walked closer and stood off to the side of the threshold of the kitchen to hear, but not too close where she would see me being nosey. I wanted to know what was going on, and this was the only way to find out. Momma was leaning into the counter with a distressed look on her face as the phone was held up to her ear by her shoulder.

"You know he can. I don't even know why you asked, Darlene. Girl, Jake. He ain't trippin' on no shit like that. Marco is family," Momma said, smacking her lips, switching the location of the phone to her other ear as she stood up. "Hold on. Bella, bring me my cigarettes off my dresser," she yelled before returning to her conversation. "I'm sorry. This shit got my nerves bad."

With no reply, I slowly stepped to the side so she wouldn't notice I was listening before making my way to her room to do as I was told. Once I got her cigarettes, I ran back to the kitchen and handed them to my mother.

"Here, Ma. We still going school shopping today?" I asked as I leaned on the counter with one hand under my chin. "Hi, Auntie Darlene. Ma, what's going on wit' Auntie and Marco?" I yelled, interjecting myself into their conversation.

"Darlene, hold on. You see me on the phone, little girl," she said, rolling her eyes. "Stay out of my conversation. We goin' to the Galleria Mall in a few, so go do your hair and brush your teeth, Bella."

"Yes, ma'am," I said, jumping back away from the counter and jetting up the stairs.

"Stop running in the house, Bella!" she yelled.

"Yes, ma'am," I replied as I disappeared into my room. Moments later, I stepped out of my room, ready to shop till Momma dropped.

After shopping, we went to get something to eat before heading back home. Pulling up to the house, we saw a silver GMC truck in the driveway. "Ma, who dat?" I was curious to know.

"I don't know," she replied with a puzzled look on her face.

"Maybe Jake got company?" I suggested.

"Chile, I don't have a clue," she said, parking in the driveway to the right of the truck. "Grab these bags, and don't forget the food," she said before turning the car off and exiting.

"Yes, ma'am," I said, quickly reaching to the back seat and grabbing my five bags and food before exiting the car. Kicking the door closed, I skipped to catch up with Momma.

"I ain't gonna tell you again about slamming my door, Bella."

"Sorry, Ma. My hands are full."

As we were getting closer to the door, we heard arguing coming from inside the house. "What the hell?" Momma said, rushing to the door to see what the commotion was all about.

"It sounds like David, Ma," I said, putting a pep in my step to remain on her heels. I wasn't going to miss a minute of what was going on in the house.

"Oh, Lord," she said, rushing into the house to find David and Jake in a heated argument.

"Nigga, you ain't nothing but a bum-ass rapist," David spat as he squared up with Jake in the kitchen.

"I can show you betta than I can tell you, li'l nigga," Jake barked.

Momma rushed in the kitchen with me hot on her heels with all my bags still in hand.

"Hold the fuck up! What's going on here?" her voice screeched.

There was nothing but silence and stares as she slammed her fist down on the counter. The tension was intense as fumes came off of both Jake and David. I froze in place, unsure of what was going on. They both stood in the kitchen, preparing to throw hands.

"Somebody better start telling me what the fuck is going on. Jake?" Ma said, standing in front of them with her face redder than a flame.

"Tell her, David. Tell yo' momma about the bricks and weed stash you had hidden in the basement. Riskin' everybody's freedom in this house."

"Naw, nigga, you tell her how you been getting that work from me for weeks," David spat back.

"You did what? Don't try to flip this on Jake," Momma yelled as tears started to fill her eyes. "Why, David?"

"I came home while he was loading it up in the truck outside," Jake yelled, pointing to the front door.

"Hold the fuck up. Bitch, so you got this bum-ass nigga over me. I don't understand why you even got him around Bella anyway?" David said as he attempted to step in her face.

Tears fell down my face as my body began to shake uncontrollably. This whole situation was hard to watch, as a chill went up my spine. David was selling drugs again. I couldn't believe it. "Ma," I yelled in terror, dropping my bags and food to the floor.

"Bella, stay back," she screamed as her hand began to form a fist. But before she could react, Jake stepped forward, placing his arm out to guide her out of the way.

Nose to nose, he now stood in front of David. "Nigga, what the fuck you say? Back the fuck up. You done lost your mind disrespecting my wife," Jake barked, giving David a shove back so quick it knocked David off his footing. "Nigga, you done lost your mind if you even think you gon' talk to her like that."

David flew back but quickly repositioned himself as he faced our mother. "You just gon' let this no-good-ass nigga put his hands on me? What kind of mother is you? He ain't gon' do nothing but use and abuse you. But hell, you ain't never been much of a mother anyway. Shid, you stayed in the bar more than at the house. You never put us first." David was spewing venomous words in her direction.

"Who the fuck are you talking to?" Momma said, stepping closer to David as she tried to move Jake's arm out of the way. "Nigga, get your ungrateful ass the fuck out, and don't come back. I'm done with you. All I have done and sacrificed for you, even after yo' dumb ass got locked up," she cried as tears ran down her cheeks.

I was frozen in place, unable to speak or move. I couldn't believe the things David was saying to Momma. This was getting way out of hand. And whose car was he driving?

David looked at me. "If you need anything, Bella, call me," he said, bending down to give me a hug.

I hugged him back. "Love you, brother," I said as we let go of each other.

I watched as he walked out the door. Even though Momma was still yelling, I couldn't seem to hear anything. It was surreal focusing on David as he got in the truck and backed out of the driveway.

"You ruined everything, Jake. I hate you!" I screamed.

"Take your ass to your room now, Bella Marie," Momma spat out.

Stomping my feet, I stormed off up the stairs, furious, slamming my bedroom door behind me. Throwing myself across my bed, I cried. "I can't believe Ma turned her back on David. I swear, I will never do my kid like that for no man."

Burying my face in my pillow, I must have dozed off.

"Bella? Bella, you up?" Marco said, opening the door and peeping his head in.

Rubbing my eyes, I rolled over. "Marco, what time is it?"

"Cuz, it's seven thirty. My mom just dropped me off."

"Welcome to death row," I said, sitting up in my bed. I was still mad about David but happy that my cousin was here.

"Damn. Bella, it's like that? Why Auntie move out here in the country?"

"Yeah, we in the straight country. And since Jake has been here, my family is falling apart. Ma changed so much, and I don't even know who she is anymore," I stated as tears left my eyes.

"Well, you got me now, cuz," Marco said, throwing his hands up.

"I guess you're right." I sniffled. "Where did she put you?"

"David's room."

"Cool," I replied, getting up to use the bathroom.

Chapter 5

Six Months Later

Saturday morning, and winter was in full swing. Marco and I sat on the couch, eating cereal as we watched cartoons while the snow was coming down outside. It was currently 12 degrees, which made the living room feel like the North Pole. We had been out of school all week due to the weather, and we were tired of sitting in the house.

"Bella, this is weak. What are we going to do now?"

"Let's walk to the gas station," I said. One thing this small town had was a gas station that was two miles from our house.

"Okay, let's go."

"Don't even worry about it." I chuckled as we both went upstairs to put on warmer clothes. Walking in my room, I put on a sweatshirt and some long, thick socks before putting on my bubble jacket.

"You ready, Bella?" Marco said, standing by my door.

"Yeah, let's go. Hold up, I gotta use the bathroom. I will meet you downstairs," I said before walking back in my room. I didn't need Marco knowing all my business because sometimes he couldn't hold water.

"Ight, hurry up."

Kneeling down on the side of my bed, I slid my hand in a small slit that I made in my mattress. This was my stash spot, just in case my mom searched my room. I had a plastic bag with a blunt that I found in the basement from David's weed stash, and a ten-dollar bill. Shoving everything in my pocket, I headed to Sammy's room to grab a lighter. Peeking out my bedroom door to make sure Marco was down the stairs, I eased out of my room and into Sammy's. Grabbing the orange lighter off his dresser, I placed it in my back pocket before heading downstairs.

"About time," Marco said, turning up his mouth. "You be taking forever to do nothing, Bella."

"Boy, hush," I said, putting on my coat and boots. "Ma, we're going to the gas station," I yelled before closing the door behind us. "Dang, it's cold as hell outside," I said, rubbing my hands together.

"Yeah, it is, I can't wait for summer, Bella. I'ma find me a girl out here to chill wit'."

"Oh, yeah!" I said, pulling the bag out of my front pocket. "You wanna smoke this blunt I found?"

Marco's eyes got big. "Hell yeah! Light it up!"

"Hold up," I said, coming to a complete stop, facing him. Holding up my right pinky, I said, "You have to swear on God you ain't gonna say shit to nobody, and I mean it, Marco."

Holding up his left pinky and looking me in my eyes, he said, "I swear I won't say nothing, cuz."

"Bet," I said, pulling the lighter out of my back pocket. I lit the blunt and took a puff.

Cough cough cough.

"Hmmm, take this," I said, waving my hand in Marco's direction.

"Hahaha," he laughed, reaching for the blunt and inhaling it deeply, causing him to cough and fold over. "Damn."

"We are both first timers, huh?" I said, patting him on the back. "You all right?"

We both started laughing as he passed back the blunt. We continued smoking and talking as we made our way to the store.

"You, high yet, Marco?" I was curious when the effects would kick in. "'Cause I can't tell."

"Shit, all I feel is the cold air hitting my ankles." He laughed while opening the door to the store.

Ding, dong.

"Welcome," the cashier said.

"Hello," we responded. A euphoric sensation took over my body, and my eyelids began to shrink as I glided through the aisles, scanning all the food. Everything looked good. Even the smell of that nasty-ass pizza they kept out by the cashier was good.

"Marco, grab some stuff too."

"Good lookin', Bella," he said, stumbling over his feet as he tried to turn around.

"Hahahaha," I laughed. *This fool high as hell*, I thought.

"What are you laughing at?" Marco chuckled.

"You! Man, get ya stuff so we can go," I said, grabbing my favorite snack, Chips Ahoy cookies and milk.

Heading to the counter, I pulled the ten-dollar bill out of my pocket and handed it to the lady as Marco placed his items on the counter too. "These too, ma'am," I said as the cashier was ringing us up.

"Is this all?" she said, chewing a wad of gum, looking me up and down before holding the money up toward the light.

"Yes, ma'am." I laughed, looking at her crooked teeth. "Can you put these in separate bags?" I said, pointing to Marco's items.

The cashier scoffed, placing his items in a separate bag.

Rolling my eyes, we grabbed our bags and walked out of the store. The walk home was tough because we froze all the way as we stomped through the snow. Snow in Barker was next level because they didn't have people to come right out and clear the roads. The snow was so heavy my steps felt like I was walking in cement. Thank goodness we didn't have far to go.

We were about a hundred feet away from the house when I stopped and turned to Marco. "Remember, don't say shit," I instructed.

"I ain't. You don't gotta keep saying that. And, cuz, I seen that shit the cashier pulled. Fuck that bitch for real. Hell, she just mad she gotta work," Marco said.

"Okay, unfortunately it's the only store in town," I said, turning my lips up.

I started to run the rest of the way to the house, making it all the way to the first step before busting my butt. I just lay there, laughing and making snow angels until Marco made it to the house to help me up.

As we walked in the house, I heard Momma call my name.

"Bella Marie, make sure y'all clean up in here," she said as she and Jake walked into the living room.

"Yes, ma'am."

"I left y'all money on the counter for food, and don't turn that heat up past seventy-three," Jake said, grabbing their coats out of the closet.

"We're taking off for a little while. We will be back later," Momma said.

We watched as they put on their winter coats and boots before leaving the house. Looking over at Marco, I rolled my eyes and whispered, "Shid, they won't be back till tomorrow if we're lucky."

Marco and I removed our winter gear and walked in the living room. We sat on the couch and watched through the window as they got into the truck and disappeared into the snowfall. Reaching up to close the curtains, I turned around, pulling my cookies and milk out of my bag.

"Hand me the remote," Marco said. Tossing me the bag, he asked, "What are we about to watch?"

"I don't know yet. What comes on tonight?" I asked, channel surfing before stopping on B.E.T. "We can watch videos."

"Coo'," Marco replied.

Smacking on my cookies, I washed it down with the milk. "Dang, Marco, I think this just brought me back to life, 'cause that weed had me messed up. How you feel?"

"I'm still hungry," he replied as his stomach began rumbling.

"Go make you some noodles or a sandwich."

"When are you gonna order the food, Bella?"

"In a little bit. It's still early."

Marco mumbled underneath his breath as he walked in the kitchen to find something to eat.

A few hours went by, and we ordered two pizzas and twenty pieces of extra crispy wings with lemon pepper. Once delivered, we started watching movies back-to-back. The first movie we chose was the classic *Texas Chainsaw Massacre*.

As the movie ended, Marco said, "What's next, Bella?"

"Umm, I don't know. Let's watch *Freddy's Dead*."

"Coo'," Marco said, putting the tape in the VCR and pressing play.

As we were getting into the movie, I glanced over at the window, seeing lights shining through the curtains. "You see that?"

"What?"

"Them lights, Marco," I replied, smacking my lips. *He never pays attention*, I thought, trying to ignore the window. We continued watching the movie. I heard a car door close, and I slightly turned to the window. I moved the curtain just a little bit so I could see. Out of nowhere, Mom's picture of Jesus's last supper just dropped from the old beige wall, straight to the floor behind the TV, causing us to jump.

"Shit!" I squealed. "Ssh ssh. Listen. You hear that?"

"What the fuck? Yeah, I do. Maybe it's Sammy?" Marco suggested.

"Dat nigga in Lockport with his girl, but it's a car in the driveway. I heard the car door close."

"Who would be all the way out here?" Marco replied.

"I don't know," I said, peeping out the curtains again now with Marco standing behind me. "Shoot. I don't see anything but lights. You see anything?" I whispered.

"Nah, just light too."

Fixing the curtains back, we suddenly heard someone knocking on the door.

"Who is it?" I yelled.

"It's me. David."

Releasing my anxiety, I opened the door and immediately hugged him. Since he had moved out, we didn't get to see much of him. David walked in wearing a red-and-white Adidas tracksuit with a matching Kangol. The chain he had on was bursting with diamonds that set off his new fancy gold teeth.

Smiling, he dapped up Marco, then asked, "Where's Moms?"

"She's not here. They left earlier," I said, still smiling from the excitement.

"Y'all wanna ride to the city with me?"

We both gave each other a look in agreement as we decided to take the chance and ride out with David. "Yeah!" we yelled in unison.

"Coo'. I'm parked in front of the house."

Marco and I threw on our winter gear and jetted out the door before David could even tell us to lock up.

We all piled into this small-ass red pickup truck. I was curious to know whose truck it was because it couldn't be David's. He just had the GMC last time I saw him. *I'm riding anyways, so what's the point in asking?* I thought as I bounced to the music.

The music was blasting as we cruised through the streets listening to the new Nas CD, *Illmatic.* We rode, vibing out as David smoked his weed, driving like a pro through the snow. I was scared and excited at the same time as we finally got into Lockport, with the roads getting even worse as we approached the city limits. Sliding all over the streets and almost spinning out a couple of times, David managed to keep control as our laughter filled the truck.

We stopped at this red house on Erie Street. He pulled into the driveway, turned down the radio, then looked over to me and Marco.

"Look, I'll be right back out. Don't touch anything. I mean that shit," David said, giving me a stern stare.

"Whatever," I replied, rolling my eyes.

We sat in the truck and watched as he walked up to the house and knocked. *Who the hell lives here?* I thought. Just then, a white man opened the door and let David in. As we sat, I turned the radio up just a tad to knock out some of that awkward silence that filled the truck. Staring out the window, nervousness took over my mind as we waited for David to return.

"I wonder who that white man is, Marco?

"Ain't no telling, cuz. Why did he look out the door like that? Did you peep that?" Marco said, stretching his neck, looking like the man.

"Yeah, I saw him. Oooweee, David better get his life together." I laughed. "I hope he hurries up while he handlin' business," I joked. "Tuh, I don't want Momma to beat us home. You know she will trip."

"Bella, you don't know what he got going on. Mind ya business." Marco laughed. "And you're right, 'cause Auntie doesn't play."

"I'm just saying."

As we continued talking, I saw the front door open, and David reappeared.

"Finally," I yelled, watching him walk out of that white man's house, smiling, with a little pep in his step.

David oddly looked up and down the street as if he was looking for someone. Once he made it back to the truck, he opened the door, jumping in. "Y'all want something to eat?"

Marco and I both yelled, "Yup."

"McDonald's it is!" he said, pulling off.

It took us about ten minutes to pull up to the drive-thru speaker. David turned the music down and ordered while reaching into his jacket pocket. Pulling out a large stack of money, David peeled off a crisp fifty-dollar bill before putting the rest back in his pocket.

"Brother, can I get some money? You balling," I said, reaching out my hand in David's direction.

"You silly as hell, Bella." He laughed, reaching back in his jacket. He peeled off two of those crispy fifties for me and Marco.

"Thanks, David," I said.

"Yeah, thanks," Marco replied.

"Your total is twelve eighty-nine. Please pull around to the first window."

What was David really doing in that man's house? I thought, placing the money in my pocket.

Once David paid, he got our food, and he took us home, bumping Nas all the way. My thoughts were racing, and I couldn't stop thinking about the money he pulled out

and how he was making that type of money. We drove
for about twenty minutes before pulling up to my house.
Seeing that the coast was clear, Marco and I grabbed our
bags and hurried inside. Once we were safe in the house,
I waved as David pulled off.

We each ran to our rooms and took off our clothes and
put on our pajamas. Heading back to the living room, we
grabbed our food and started to watch television. I pondered on my thoughts all night. From that day forward,
I knew money would change my life. I just didn't know
how to get it.

The following morning, I woke up in a great mood,
replaying our night with David. But my thoughts were
quickly drowned out by my mom's screaming.

"Bella Marie! Girl, do you hear me?"

As I opened my door, the smell of stale cigarettes
instantly hit my nostrils. "Yeah, Ma," I called out.

"Don't yeah me, girl. Come see what I want."

On my way downstairs, I went to wake up Marco. *If I'm
in trouble, then so is he*, I thought, opening the door and
peeking my head inside.

"I'm coming," he said as he put on his socks before I
could even speak.

Looking across to Sam's room, I saw his door wide
open and the bed still neatly made. *I hope he will be back
tonight. He has been with that chick way too long*, I
thought as I headed downstairs.

My brother was fine. He rocked a perfectly sculpted
fro that always seemed to glisten in the sunlight. He was
Dad's twin with the exact features. His brown eyes and
light cocoa skin made him a hood chick's weakness.

"Yeah, come in." Marco's voice barked at me.

"Dang, you good?" I asked.

"Yeah, what's up, Bell?"

"You wanna walk to the gas station?" I said.

"What, you got another blunt?" He laughed. "Auntie gon' kill us if she even thinks she smells some weed."

"Shut up. Do you wanna go or not?"

"Of course. Let's roll," he said. "What Auntie want?" he asked.

"Not sure. I'm 'bout to go see," I said, making my way downstairs. "Hurry up, Marco," I yelled from the bottom of the stairs before walking into the kitchen.

The first thing I noticed was Jake's ass sitting at the kitchen table with a non-filtered cigarette hanging out of his mouth, mumbling some shit. Looking over at my mom's beet red face, I could tell this would not go well.

"Yes, ma'am?"

"Where is Marco's ass?"

"He's comin'," I said as Marco entered the kitchen.

"Why didn't y'all clean up my shit?" she yelled, staring a hole right through the both of us.

I looked over at Marco, who was pinching the side of his sweats and holding a very nervous look on his face. I knew he would have folded up under pressure as soon as I had left the room.

Thinking quickly on my feet, I rubbed my eyes and spoke. "I fell asleep, Ma. Sorry."

"Get my shit cleaned up," she said.

"Yes, ma'am," I said, walking to the kitchen sink to start doing the dishes.

"I got the living room," Marco said.

"I don't care what y'all do, just clean my house up," Ma snapped.

I stacked the dishes before I started to wash. Filling up the sink with hot water and dish soap, I then started scraping the rest of that mac and cheese pan in the trash so I could put some water in it to soak. I found myself drifting off and thinking about how I could make money like David. Whatever he was doing, it seemed to be working just fine for him.

"Ma, David came by looking for you last night."

"Why? He knows I don't mess wit' him after that situation went down. What did he want?"

"I don't know. He didn't tell me. It was nice to see him though, Ma."

"Well, it couldn't be that important," she said, lighting her cigarette.

"Here, Bella. Where do you want these couple of cups at?" Marco asked.

"Put them on the counter," I replied.

Once we finished cleaning and went upstairs to my room, I pulled out the fifty David gave me. "Shit, he back selling crack!" I yelled. It all made sense now—the truck, the strange white man. With this revelation, I immediately headed to tell Marco.

When I knocked on the door, I heard him let out a heavy sign before saying, "Come in."

"Fuck is wrong wit' you? You ready to go to the gas station?"

We headed downstairs, grabbing our coats and boots out of the closet. After throwing our gear on, we headed to the gas station. At first, our conversation was about some random things, then, out of the blue, Marco said, "You know, I'm thinking about going into the army when I turn eighteen."

"Oh, you really leaving me too?"

"I gotta try to do something different, and my mom don't want me to live with her no way. Bella, I'm seventeen. You see, I've been living with y'all since I was sixteen."

"Don't say it like that. Yeah, Ma gotchu, but Auntie gotchu too. She is just going through it right now," I said, sucking my teeth.

"I ain't saying it like that," Marco said, putting his head down as he kicked a pile of snow. "I wanna do something with my life, Bella. Something different."

"You know you are my favorite cousin, right? And I gotcha too. So, whatever you decide to do, I'm witchu."

Marco paused, looking up at me with a smile. "Yeah, I know."

As we got closer to the gas station, I yelled, "Last one to the door pays!" as I sprinted past him.

Chapter 6

Two Years Later

My mom and Jake bought their first house in Wrights Corners, a small town right outside of Lockport city limits. It wasn't the city, but it was one step closer to civilization for me. We were still one of the only Black families in town. At seventeen, I had developed anxiety, probably from being out in the country for so long. I was ready for a change.

The house was a lot smaller than the house in Baker, but Momma didn't care because she was officially a homeowner. The water-blue house had four bedrooms with two bathrooms. It was smaller than the old house. I didn't have a bathroom in my room, but with Sammy never home, it was still like having my own bathroom. We had been there about a month, and I was able to catch up with my old friends, especially Kayla. I even saw David more often with us living closer to the city now.

After finishing up my chores, I decided to walk to the Strangers to get some snacks. Running upstairs, I quickly changed, throwing on a pair of shorts, T-shirt, and gym shoes, then headed to the store. Marco was visiting his mom for the weekend, so I had to go to the store by myself. It was crazy hot outside as I walked down Lake Ave.

After about thirty minutes, I arrived at Strangers, which was inside Lockport city limits. I walked inside the store, grabbing some Mary Janes, chips, and a juice before heading to the counter to pay. Mrs. Margaret was bending over, counting the cigarette inventory.

"Hey, Mrs. Margaret," I said, placing my items on the counter.

"Hey, Bella, is that all you gettin', sweetie?" she said, rising from the floor.

"Yes, ma'am," I said, handing her my money and grabbing my bag off the counter.

"Tell your mother I said hello," she said as she continued the inventory.

"Yes, ma'am," I said as I walked out of the store. My brother's David's friend Bryce was walking in.

"Aww, shit. Hey, Bella, what are you doing up here?"

"Grabbing some snacks. 'Bout to head back home."

"Damn, that's about a thirty-minute walk. You want a ride back to the house?" he said, shaking his head.

"Heck yeah. Thank you." I smiled.

"It's coo'. Let me grab a few things and I'll be right out. I'm parked right there in the blue Cadillac out front," he said as he walked into the store.

Leaning on his car, I waited for about five minutes before Bryce walked out of the store. Just as he opened my door for me to get in, David pulled up and jumped out of the car, on ten.

"Da fuck is you doing, Bella?" he barked. "Why the fuck are you getting in this nigga car?" he said, lighting into me.

"Whatchu mean? Why are you so mad?" I cried, running back into the store. I had never been called so many bitches and whores in my life.

"Mrs. Margaret. Mrs. Margaret. Can you please call my mom? David is outside trippin'." I sniffled, wiping my eyes.

"What? Yes, baby," Mrs. Margaret replied. "Kevin, come watch the counter," she yelled before going to the back to call my mom.

It didn't take Momma long before she pulled up in front of the store. I watched for her out the store window. When she walked through the front door, my eyes instantly filled with tears.

"Bella, you okay?" she asked, coming in the door.

With no reply, I shook my head and cried. I could not understand why David went off on me the way he did. He treated me like I wasn't his sister.

"Thank you, Margaret. Come on, Bella. Let's go," Momma said as we walked out of the store hand and hand.

"Get in the car," Momma said, walking over to the driver's side to get in.

I got in the car, and the investigation started. My mom was a star investigator.

"Tell me what the fuck happened, Bella," she yelled, banging on the steering wheel.

As tears streamed down my face, it was difficult to catch my breath. I took short breaths between words. "Dave. Just. Cussed. Me. Out," I cried, taking two slow, deep breaths to calm down and get my next sentence out. "Ma, he was calling me all types of bitches and whores," I whined as more tears filled my eyes.

Suddenly, Momma pulled off at top speed, making a left on Lock Street. Her facial muscles were tight, and her cheek color changed to a slight tinge of red. Slamming on the brakes, she put the car in park. "Muthafucka," she mumbled. "Stay here, Bella," she ordered, jumping out of the car. She left the engine running and never closed the door behind her.

Looking around, I felt a nervous energy shoot through my body when I saw her walk up to David, who was sitting on his friend Benny's porch, smoking weed. She walked up as David was getting ready to pass a bottle of brown liquor, slapping it out of his hand before he could hand it off. As the bottle hit the ground, he looked up at Momma.

Her arms flared in the air back and forth as she screamed, "What the fuck is your problem?"

Rolling down the window, I thought, *This 'bout to be good.* I leaned over to hear every word.

"David. Why you disrespecting her like—?"

"But . . . but, Ma," he said, cutting her off.

"Don't you cut me off, muthafucka. That is my child, and you bet not *evvva* in yo' life talk to her like that again," she said before he could finish his sentence.

That's what the fuck he gets, I thought as a wicked grin formed on my face.

David turned beet red from embarrassment. Standing up, he yelled, "But, Ma, she was getting in Bryce's car. You know he likes them girls young."

"She was what?" Mom yelled, looking back at me with a tense glare before turning her attention back on David. "She's still your sister, and you ain't got no right to fuckin' talk to her like that," she spat.

"Yes, ma'am," he replied, lowering his head as she walked off and got back in the car.

Looking over at me as her nostrils flared, she tossed the car in drive and peeled off.

"Stay yo' li'l ass out of these niggas' cars," she said, smacking her lips.

"Yes, ma'am," I said as we drove home in silence. I was scared even to breathe wrong because I knew I would be next if I said or did the wrong thing.

Once we made it back to the house, she went straight to her room, slamming the door behind her without uttering another word. Marco was back from visiting his mom and was sitting on the couch, watching TV.

"Bro, what the fuck?" he asked.

"Man, it's a long story. I will tell you later," I said heading upstairs to my room.

Two weeks had passed since the incident with David, and Momma had been staying down my throat over petty shit. Marco had decided to move back in with his mom and had been gone a week now, so it was just me in the house. Sammy moved out with his girlfriend a few months earlier, so I hadn't seen much of him.

I got up and began cleaning up before going to hang with my friends. I knew that asking to go out without my chores done was out of the question. As I finished up the kitchen, Jake walked in, standing next to me as he leaned on the counter, his breath smelling like stale beer.

"Let's go fishing at the Canal. We can even have a few drinks." He smirked, grabbing and twisting a strand of my hair around his index finger. He had a creepy glare in his eyes as he waited for my answer.

Taken aback, I cocked my head to the side so he would release my hair. "Umm, nah. I'm good." I frowned as I turned up the corner of my lip.

Did he just try me? I thought as I finished up the dishes. His whole vibe wasn't sitting well with me.

Just then, Momma walked in the kitchen, looking at me crazy as if I did something wrong. Jake immediately backed away from the counter and sat at the kitchen table.

"What the fuck you doin'?" she asked as her eyes shift from me to him.

"Maybe you should ask your husband," I said, smacking my lips before turning and walking off to my room. All I could do was sit on my bed and cry. Moments later, I heard my mother and Jake arguing.

I am too old to let anyone think they can violate me, I thought as tears fell down my cheeks.

Just then, she stormed into my room with hell in her eyes. "Bella, how many times I gotta tell you not to wear those little bitty-ass shorts around the house with no bra?"

"Huh?" I said, wiping my tears with my arm. "Why you yelling at me? He was the one trying to get me to go to the canal with him and drink," I spat, annoyed that she was somehow blaming me.

"He would never do that!" she yelled. "I know you don't like him, Bella, but don't lie on him," she said before walking out and slamming the door behind her. The way she just looked at me as she walked out of my room had me pissed.

I didn't know where I was going, but I was leaving today. I grabbed my Guess backpack, and I started gathering my things, throwing my sneakers and clothes in the backpack. I was so tired of this. Picking up my phone, I called my homegirl Rain, who recently found a spot in the Falls, to see if I could crash there for a few days.

"Hello, Rain?"

"Bella?"

"Yeah, girl, it's me. I was wondering if I could come crash at your spot for a little bit. My mom is buggin', girl."

"You already know you good, but I'm out in the Falls, so you will have to get a ride here."

"Bet. Let me figure out a ride. I'ma call you when I'm on the way."

"Okay, girl. I'll see you in a minute," Rain said before hanging up.

Scanning my little black phone numbers, I searched to see I could call for a ride. "Nah, she's at work," I said, flipping to the next page. "Shid, ain't no way he's gon' take me without being in my business," I mumbled. "Fuck it. Let me call a cab."

Grabbing my backpack, I took one last look around my room, making sure I didn't forget anything before walking downstairs to grab the phone book. I heard Momma and Jake leave, most likely to go to the bar, so I didn't have to worry about them. Grabbing the phone receiver, I pulled the cord, stretching it all the way to the table, and sat down. Placing the phone book on the table, I flipped through the pages to find a cab.

"Union Cab, what's the address?"

"Umm, I have a question."

"What is it?" the voice said, sounding irritated.

"How much to go to Niagara Falls from this address?" I asked.

"Hold," the man said. After a brief wait, the man yelled out, "Twenty-five dollars, sweetheart. Do you want it?"

"Yes."

"Thirty minutes," he told me before slamming the phone in my ear.

"Dickhead," I mumbled, getting up and hanging up the phone. Slightly turning my head, I checked the time on the microwave.

"Dang, I gotta call Rain." I sighed, picking the phone back up. Just as I dialed her number, putting the receiver to my ear, Momma walked in.

"Hello. I will be there in like forty minutes. I'm taking a cab."

"Okay. When you get here, come to the side door and walk in."

"Okay. Thanks again, Rain. I'ma see you in a minute."

When I hung up the phone, Momma was looking at me, shaking her head and puffing on a full-flavored cigarette. She exhaled, blowing out a puff of smoke "G'on and be grown. Just don't come back to my shit pregnant."

"I ain't you," I said, brushing past her and going into my room.

Snatching my hair, she yanked my head back as she pulled me toward her. "Who the fuck do you think you are? You think you're going to disrespect me in my house? I had you, you little bitch. You ain't have me," she screamed, dragging me in the hall, then randomly smacking me in my face and head. Her breath smelled like a whole bottle of gin.

"Get off of me, you crazy lady," I screamed, blocking her arm from hitting my face again as we were tussling in the hallway before Jake pulled her off of me.

"What's going on here?" Jake yelled.

"This bitch is disrespectful, and I'm not going for it," she screamed.

Without saying another word, I grabbed my bag and walked out the front door. As the door closed, I heard Jake say, "Let her go. She will be back."

Moments later, the cab pulled up. I hopped in, vowing never to return.

Looking out the window as we drove down 104, I couldn't get over Momma putting her hands on me. *How could she put her hands on me like that? She's no better than David,* I thought. I didn't know what was worse—mental or physical abuse. Either way, I wasn't tolerating it anymore.

After forty-five minutes, the cab pulled in front of Rain's house.

"That will be twenty-five dollars," he said, opening the palm of his right hand.

Reaching in my backpack, I pulled out my wallet and handed him $30. "Keep the change," I said, placing my wallet back in my backpack before opening the door and getting out.

I paused for a moment, taking in my new surroundings. Inhaling deeply, I took the first steps into my future. I was ready for the world. No rules, no curfew.

Rain was a real chill white chick who dated Sammy. She graduated last year, but we had been cool since we moved back closer to Lockport. She was shaped like another chick from the hood, with big-ass titties to match her big-ass hips. All the dope boys liked her because she used to allowed them to trap out her spot from time to time.

Rain stayed in the middle of the hood. The dark brick building reminded me of a prison. I followed her directions and entered the house. She was in the living room, rolling up on the couch.

"Hey, Rain."

"Hey, Bella," she said, licking the blunt. "Make yourself at home. Your room is on the left."

It was a perfect spot for a D-boy who was trying to get money. Rain had a cool little spot. There were three rooms and a bathroom upstairs, a nice-size kitchen and living room. I put my things down in the room and joined her on the couch.

Passing me the blunt, she said, "Tell me what the fuck went down."

"Girl, you know how my momma can get when she is drunk," I said.

"Not again."

"Yeah, I told her about her husband, and she seems to blame me for his actions. Talking about wearing some little shorts, Rain."

"That's fucked up for real. You're her daughter."

"Right." I inhaled the blunt, hoping it would take away my problems.

"You gonna pass that?" Rain pointed out.

"Oh, shit, yeah! Here you go. My bad," I said, laughing.

"You were in deep thought for a second. You okay?" Rain asked.

"Yeah, I am just glad you're letting me crash here. I can't believe my mom for real, Rain."

"That's what friends are for, right?" she said in an eerie tone. There was something about the way she said it, like she had a motive.

"Rain, do you have anything to drink?"

Getting up, she walked to the fridge. "Water or juice?"

"Juice, please."

Walking back in the living room, she handed me the cup.

"Thanks," I said after I wet my palate.

"You're welcome." Sitting at the other end of the couch, she turned on the radio.

Easing my thoughts just a little, we continued talking for hours about everything that had transpired in the last few weeks as we passed the blunt back and forth for the rest of the night. I passed out right where I was sitting on the couch, not even realizing that I was that exhausted from everything that had happened.

Chapter 7

I needed some fresh air, so I decided to walk to the store to get a full glimpse of the neighborhood. There was no doubt about it. I was in the middle of the hood. The houses were dilapidated, and some of the apartments were boarded up with bright green citation tickets sticking on the doors. Walking down the block, I hit a right at the corner, continuing straight. Looking up halfway down the block, I saw the store that sat on the corner. I approached the small blue building that had Newport and beer advertisements all over it, covering up the old paint. There were PLAY LOTTO posters on the doors that had a metal fence for extra protection. Inside, it smelled of fried chicken and cheap incense.

I picked up what I needed quickly as the smell had my nostrils flaring, turning my stomach from that cheap incense. I got up out of there and headed back to the house. More than halfway down the block, I heard this voice as I was trying to keep it copacetic in this 98-degree weather with no wind. The sun was beating down on me, causing my eyes to squint. Looking up and across the street, I tried to focus my eyes on the voice.

"Yo! Yo, li'l momma."

I turned in his direction, glaring with no response. *This nigga must think I'm one of the trending hoes from the hood,* I thought, cocking my head to the side.

"Yo! What's ya name?" he asked from the yellow house that sat on the corner.

"Who, me?" I said, pointing my finger at my chest.

"Yeah, you," he said, coming from behind the metal fence and walking toward me.

Switching my bag to my alternate hand, I felt a nervous chill fill my body the closer he got. "Can I help you?"

"What's good, ma?" he said with a slight smile. "They call me T, but my name is Tyrell. Wuz yo' name?"

"Bella Marie."

"You wanna smoke?" he offered, pulling a blunt from behind his ear and lighting it. His bright green eyes glittered in the sunlight, allowing his high cheekbones to complement his amazing mocha-swirled skin. He had a fresh edge-up that made his deep waves stand out.

Oh my God, I thought, still playing hard to get. "Naw, maybe another time." I smiled as the smell of his cologne took over the air. I took a deep breath, and his scent caused my pussy to jump. Slowly, I turned to walk off, but midway down the block I stopped and glanced over my shoulder.

This muthafucka still watching me walk away. Immediately, I started switching my ass with power and precision, arching my back a little as my hips swayed from left to right while I continued back to the house.

That night, I was in my room and couldn't stop smiling, thinking about him. His features stood out, along with his unique swag. *That nigga was too fine*, I thought as an electrifying energy shot through my body, causing my pussy to moisten. This man was different and so well put together. The vivid thoughts of our possible future encounters made my pussy throb with excitement. Sliding my fingers inside my panties, I explored my passion box and wondered what his touches would feel like against my warm body. This was big for me. After being molested multiple times growing up, sex was always something I tried to avoid. But Tyrell was bringing something out of me that I could not control.

The following day, I walked back to the store, hoping to see him again. I grabbed a pop and a bag of chips then headed to the front counter to check out.

"Bella Marie. What up, cutie?" he said, licking his lips.

"Tyrell, right?" I smiled.

"Yeah. You tryin' to smoke today, li'l momma?" He laughed.

"Aye, actually we can." I smiled as my eyes scanned his well-built body.

"Hold up," he told the cashier as he grabbed a beer from the cooler. "I'm paying for all this," he said, grabbing the bags with one hand and guiding me out the store with the other hand on my lower back.

"My truck is just over there," he said, pointing to a money-green Range Rover with chrome rims.

It was clean as fuck. We rode around, smoking and listening to this new rapper that was playing on the radio.

"This shit fire," Tyrell said, nodding his head to the beat.

"Hell yeah," I said, bobbin' my head.

"Shid, I hear he's a white boy outta Detroit," he said, passing me the blunt.

As we continued to ride through the city, I let my guard down just a little as he took his time to get to know me. I was young and just as green as a two-dollar bill, and he knew it.

Within a few weeks, Tyrell was consuming the majority of my time. It felt like I had known him my entire life. It was weird because I never had someone show me attention without expectations. Tyrell had so much confidence in himself that it made him even more attractive. Since childhood, I had never experienced any man that had it all together. Even the ones Momma dated were all bums leeching off of her, never pouring into her. Tyrell was willing to come into my life and make me better.

Tyrell put me up on mannerism. He got me to notice habits, quirks, and most importantly, people's characteristics. I soaked it up like a sponge.

He would always tell me, "Presence is an essence, baby girl." He was always finessing his words to get what he wanted. With a quiet transition, I was at a level I wanted to be at. He kept me mesmerized by his actions, showing me that with my looks and playing this game correctly, I could have whatever I wanted whenever I wanted it.

In order to seduce the world, I needed money to play the game, so I'd gotten a li'l job at Burger King and took up GED classes to collect this SSI money from my dad, which was right on time. They were both right down the street from the house but in opposite directions. I made enough money to get what I needed and save toward buying a car. Tyrell pretty much took care of everything else when I asked, but I barely had to. I was falling hard for this man because he loved me in a way that I had never experienced. I didn't want or need for anything. He provided.

Five Months Later

I hadn't seen or spoken to Tyrell for the last couple of days due to work and school. I was determined to have my own car and apartment by the summertime. I was tired as hell walking into a dimly lit house, with slow jams echoing through the house.

Oh, damn, this bitch got a li'l boo thang over, I thought, slowly tiptoeing down the hallway so I didn't disturb their groove session. As I passed by the kitchen, I froze, not believing what I was seeing in the kitchen area. Rain was on her knees in front of my man, sucking his dick, butt-ass naked.

"You slut-ass bitch," I spat, snatching her by the hair and dragging into the living room while punching her in the face. "Bitch! You funky-ass bitch!" I yelled with every swing.

"Bella!" He laughed, pulling me off of her. "Why you trippin'? This ain't shit. We could have enjoyed her together. You buggin', yo."

"I'm sorry. He made me do it, Bella," she cried, crawling in the corner.

Stepping back, disgusted by his words, I yelled, "Naw, fuck you and this dirty bitch." Immediately running to my room and slamming the door, I started packing all my shit, feeling stupid as tears ran down my eyes from the betrayal of the two people I trusted the most. Tyrell was my first everything, and for him to violate me in this way was unforgivable. "I should've known better than to think I was any different from the rest of his bitches," I mumbled. "Fuck! Fuck!" I screamed at the top of my lungs, shaking my head as anger and despair took over my thoughts.

I will never make the same mistake twice. Lesson learned, I thought, wiping my tears.

Devastated by the whole situation, I made the one phone call I said I was never going to make in life. With no clear choice, I started to dial the number, but every time I got to the last two digits, I would hang up. There were no words that I could think of to say at that moment.

"Shit!" I cried, feeling defeated. I finally made the call. Looking up, I noticed a picture of me and Tyrell on the dresser. I wanted to kill his motherfucking ass. The tears streamed as I called home.

"Hello?"

"Ma," I cried as a feeling of shame ran through my body.

"Bella? Are you okay?"

Hearing the concern in her voice caused my tears to pour out, and I told her what happened immediately.

"What the hell?" she yelled.

"I'm in the Falls."

"Is that bitch still there? Fuck that. Give me the address, and I'm coming to pick you up."

"Two four one three Ashland Avenue."

"I'm on my way. It's gon' be okay."

I hung up the phone, grabbed my bags, and walked out of the room. As I passed the living room, there were no signs of Rain or Tyrell. I walked out of the house and headed downstairs to wait for my mom. Sitting on the bottom step, I cried, still in disbelief of everything that had happened. About an hour later, my mom pulled up in her sweats, gym shoes, and her hair in a bun.

Rolling her window down, she asked, "You got everything? Put your stuff in the trunk."

"Yes, ma'am," I said as she popped the truck. Placing my bags inside, I walked over to the passenger side and hopped in the car. With no further questions, she pulled off at top speed.

Part of the way home was in silence. After a while, Mom spoke in the softest tone I have ever heard.

"We all have to learn one way or the other about love and relationships, especially the ones that are not meant for us to pursue, baby. I'm sorry this has to be your lesson," she said, wiping tears from her face.

My mom's words cut deep as we continued to ride in silence the rest of the way. When we pulled into the driveway, I realized being apart from my mom had been hard for me. I got out of the car and grabbed my stuff from the trunk. There was an uneasy vibe as I walked through the front door. I knew that I wasn't going to last long here.

Walking in the house, I saw Jake sitting on the couch, drinking a beer and smoking a cigarette. Looking over at me, he said, "So, Bella, what's your next move? How long do you plan on staying this time?"

"Don't start with her, Jake," my mother said, coming through the door behind me. "Bella, go and put your things up, baby."

I knew it wouldn't be long before he had something to say, I thought, rolling my eyes as I walked to my old room. I didn't bother to reply to his sarcasm.

Being in my old room brought on a surreal feeling. I let out a heavy sigh as I flung my things on the floor. Flopping down on my bed, all I could do was bury my face in my pillow as tears began to flow. "This is what I get for being caught up in my feelings. I should've been on my toes like my brothers taught me. Fuck!" I mumbled, shaking my head at my stupidity. Tyrell played me, and it crushed my soul, but I wouldn't forget the lesson he taught me.

"Pull your shit together and chalk up this loss, bitch," I mumbled, wiping my face.

Two Months Later

"Hello," I answered, putting the finishing touches on my makeup.

"Hey, bitch. Whatcha doing tonight?" Brandy asked, popping her gum multiple times.

"Hey, girl! Nothing. Whatcha got up?" I asked, ready to turn the fuck up. Brandy was cool and was always the life of the party. Every street nigga from Lockport, Niagara Falls, and Buffalo knew Brandi.

"Shid, let's get up with ol' boy and his friend then?"

"Who? Where are we going?" I asked, unsure of her motives. After dealing with Tyrell and Rain's asses, I wasn't taking any chances.

"Bitch, Choppa and Pugg! You down?"

"Yeah!" I said, looking for the fastest escape out of this emotional roller coaster I was experiencing.

"Bitch! The hood niggas is outside. We'll be there by ten to pick you up."

"Okay, coo'. See you in a minute." I laughed before I hung up.

A few hours passed before they picked me up. I walked out of the house to see a sparkling tan box Chevy on all Gold 26s, with tan custom interior on the seats and doors. "Oh, shit, they snapped with this," I said as I opened the passenger side rear door. "Okay, bitch," I whispered so only Brandy could hear me.

"Bella, these are my folks, Choppa and Pugg," she said, introducing me to them. I had heard her talk about them, but this was my first time hanging out with them.

"'Sup," Pugg said, looking back and nodding his head.

"Wuzzup, Bella," Choppa said, gripping the wheel. "Yo, you smoke?" he asked.

"Hell yeah. Shid." I laughed.

"Coo'. My nigga 'bout to roll up," he said, pulling off.

We drove around the city, smoking purp and listening to music before ending up at a cheap motel on the boulevard strip. *Oh, hell no*, I thought, giving Brandy the side eye. I didn't know these niggas well enough for all that.

"We in room thirty-six," Choppa told Pugg as he handed him the room key.

Oh, hell naw. These hood boogas ain't for me. Brandy slippin' on her shit with these scrubs, I thought, shaking my head.

Once in the room, I limited my drink intake and just peeped the scene. After a while, Brandy and Choppa disappeared into the bathroom. She made sure to check on me from time to time, but I knew she was in there getting high and fuckin'. Pugg didn't say much to me. He was too busy counting his money, which was cool wit' me. I just remained quiet, babysiting my drink and watching television. I was not impressed with either of these niggas.

Rolling up a blunt, I kicked my feet up on the side of the bed. I took a deep pull of this gas, trying to relax a little while as I waited for Brandy. I was ready to go, but I knew my mom wasn't going to come to get me at this time of night. Moments later, Pugg's phone started ringing, and he answered it on the fourth ring.

Five minutes later after he wrapped up his call, he knocked on the bathroom door and got no reply. Knocking again, he said, "Yo, I'm taking off. Where da keys, nigga?"

"A'ight. They on the table. Be safe, my nigga," Choppa yelled from behind the bathroom door.

Pugg grabbed the keys and his coat, looking over at me. "Nice meeting you, Bella."

"Likewise, Pugg," I replied, sipping my drink. Once he left the room, I kicked my shoes off. *Right on time*, I thought, crawling in one of the beds, smoking my blunt as I continued to watch some television. Brandy's moans got louder, echoing through the room.

Tuning her out, I eventually drifted off, until I was woken by the feeling of something on my inner thigh. Opening my eyes, I saw it was Choppa and quickly pushed his hands off me. "Nigga, you got me fucked up!" I yelled as Choppa stepped back from the bed with a just towel around his waist.

"It's coo', shorty. I was looking for keys."

"Yo, keys? Nigga, they ain't between my motherfuckin' legs. Matter of fact, you let ya boy take the car a few hours ago. Do you think I'm stupid? Brandy!" I screamed, preparing for things to get outta hand quickly.

Suddenly, the bathroom door swung open, and Brandy came out of the bathroom, dripping wet, wrapped in a towel. Her pupils were bigger than the moon. She was so high.

Feeling my face getting warmer, I said, "Take me home, now!"

"It's coo', ma. We gotta wait on Pugg to get back anyway," Choppa said, rubbing his dick print through the towel.

Knowing that Brandy was high and tricking with this nigga, I guess he thought I was about that life too. "Oh, you got me fucked up. Fuck that. Call that nigga now. I'm ready to go," I yelled, pointing my finger in the air. "Get dressed, bitch. We 'bout to go," I ordered Brandy.

"Oh, you trippin', girl," he said, grabbing his phone off the nightstand and sending a text.

Fifteen minutes later, Pugg showed up like he just rolled outta bed. I didn't care, though, because it was time to go.

When we finally made it back to Brandy's house, I went straight to bed because Brandy's ass was too fucked up for me to even cuss her out. The next day, Brandy started to apologize before I could even say anything.

"Girl, I'm sorry about last night," she slurred, still sounding drunk.

Rolling my eyes, I said, "It's cool, but I'm not hanging out with them niggas ever again." I knew I was done with Brandy too. "Umm, can you see if your dad can take me home now?"

"I'm sure he will. Let me ask him," she said as she headed into her parents' room.

"Nah, I can't hang with the bitch no more," I mumbled, grabbing my coat and purse.

Brandy stayed on Orange Port Road, and that was too far for me to walk. Facing my mom when I got home already had my nerves bad.

Her dad agreed to take me home, and I walked out of the house behind him without saying a word to Brandy. When her dad dropped me off, I walked into a dark house. The drapes were closed, but I could hear the television playing in the distance from my mom's room. I knew they were home because their cars were in the driveway. Trying not to get noticed, I tried to walk past their door straight to my room, but I failed to notice my mom until it was too late.

"Well, well, look what the cat dragged in," she barked.

"Hi, Ma," I said in a low tone.

"I thought you weren't staying out all night."

"I didn't mean to stay out. Brandy's dad was gone, and he didn't come home until this morning."

"Mm-hmm," she replied as her head tilted to the side.

I could hear the tension in her voice and knew she was not happy. Jake's bandwagon ass walked out of the room and started adding his two cents. Tuning him out, I just walked into my room before he could finish his sentence, pretending as if I didn't hear him.

Shutting my bedroom door, I threw my purse on my dresser and coat on the floor before laying across the bed. Getting lost in my thoughts, I replayed the events of last night.

"It's time to change things in my life," I mumbled before drifting off.

Chapter 8

Momma and I did a little running around in Lockport. She had a couple of doctor's appointments, and I needed to get new hair products along with some personal hygiene stuff. It was that time of month.

"Where are you trying to go, Bella?"

"Can we go by Ames and maybe Kmart?"

"Yes, but when we get done, I'ma need to fill up the tank."

"Bet, Ma," I said as she pulled out of the doctor's office, heading to Ames. "Yeah, Ma, have you talked to David or Sammy lately?

"Bella, you know damn well me and David ain't speaking. Sammy comes and goes as he pleases," she said, turning into the parking lot.

I didn't say anything. Getting out of the car, I shut my door while I waited for Ma to come from the other side so we could walk together. "Ma, where are you going to be? I'ma be where the hair products are."

"Okay. I will be a little bit everywhere. I need a few things."

"I will just come find you when I get done."

Walking in, Ma went straight, and I turned right—right into my nigga Rico.

"Wuzzup, Rico?" I smiled, looking over the at the nigga he was chillin' wit.

Oh, that muthafucka is fine, I thought, leaning over to Rico. "Who is that?" I whispered, trying to find out who his six-foot-two friend was.

"That my uncle Deion. You wanna get at him?" he replied with a mischievous look on his face. "Yo, Unc," Rico called out.

"Wuz good, nephew?" his uncle said, walking over to us as his dark brown eyes roamed my body.

"This is my homegirl, Bella," Rico said, making an introduction.

"Nice to meet you, Bella." Deion slightly nodded his head in approval at Rico. He didn't seem like the type that wanted to attract attention. He had that mysterious bad-boy swag to him, wearing a simple white tee with a pair of Black MCM jeans and a pair of classic all-white Uptowns.

His baritone voice sent chills up my spine. "Likewise." I smiled, intrigued by his smoothness.

Deion spoke a few words, appearing to be calm-natured, maybe even too calm. I remembered always hearing Momma and her sisters saying, "It's them quiet ones you have to watch out for."

This a slick nigga right here, I thought, watching him pick out a pack of white tees off the shelf.

"Rico, make sure you give Deion my number." Looking over at him, I smiled. "I gotta go, Rico," I said.

"Ight, Bella. You already know I gotcha." Rico said, reaching in for a hug.

It was a few days later when he called. By the time the third ring came in, I picked up. "Hello."

"Bella?"

"Speaking," I said, clearing my throat. "Deion?"

"Yeah, you busy?" he asked.

"Naw, what's up?"

"I am trying to see where your head's at."

"Word. What would you like to know?"

As we continued talking over the next few nights, we seemed to get more comfortable, so over the next few weeks, I found any reason to go to the city to see him. I hooked his nephew up with my homegirl Brandy. Yeah, I know she did some fucked-up shit in the past, but she also was a hood nigga magnet with a big mouth.

"Bitch, what you got up?" Brandy asked.

"'Bout to get dressed and go to the hood. Why? Wuzzup?" I replied, curious why she was asking.

"You going to fuck with Deion? If so, let me put you up on game now," she said, filling me in on the bullshit she learned while she was out with Rico.

"So, he lives wit' this bitch or what?" I asked.

"From what Rico told me, they be trappin' out of her house. But bitch, you know what the fuck is up, cuz ain't no bitch just letting a nigga trap out her shit unless they fuckin'," Brandy said, popping her gum.

"Good looking out, B. I knew his fine ass has bitches around. Well, check it. I'm about to finish getting dressed. I will see you in a few," I said, not wanting to react while she was on the phone. I can't lie; this information had me fucked up.

Knowing that he had a possible chick, I decided his hand would reveal itself in time. All I could do was play my position like Tyrell taught me. I didn't know what the situation was, and we were just friends at this point. Throwing my hair up in a ponytail, I threw on the cutest outfit I could find. Momma and Jake were gone for the weekend at the casino, so I had the house to myself.

I headed to the city and met up with Brandy and Rico on the block. Brandy and I were leaning on Rico's car, chopping it up, when she raised her eyebrows and nodded her head, alerting me that Deion was approaching.

Pulling my lip gloss out of my front pocket, I rolled some on my bottom lip, then moved my lips together to move it around. Just as I was placing my lip gloss back in my pocket, Deion walked up behind me.

"'Sup, ladies? Yo, Rico, let me holla at you?" he said, waving Rico off to the side.

"Hey, Deion," Brandy and I said in unison, continuing our conversation.

A few moments later, Deion said, "Yo, Bella, take a ride with me."

"Okay," I said as butterflies turned in my belly. "Brandy, I will holla atchu. Ight, Rico." I waved as I followed Deion to his car.

Deion wasn't flashy like the other hood niggas with a pimped-out ride. He was laid back but rode a classic all black old school Impala. No bells or whistles, but it was real clean.

Deion opened my door and waited for me to climb inside. He then walked over to the driver's side and slid in the car. By this time, the butterflies in my stomach were swimming with excitement.

Oh, shit. Just say calm, Bella, I thought as a smile appeared on my face.

Deion turned to me, scanning my body over, and smiled. "How you, beautiful?" he said, licking his lips.

Just then, nervousness took over, and I started to giggle. "I'm fine." I smiled.

"Look at you tryin' to come over to the wild side," Deon said as he pulled off.

A smile froze on my face as I replied. "You know, I'm curious. I ain't gon' lie. I be watchin' you make your moves here and there. I didn't know you was diggin' me like that."

"Shid, I like yo' vibe. But I wasn't trying to be that nigga. I spoke to my nephew about you and shit when I peeped you out. He said you was cool peoples," Deion said, gripping the wheel.

"Oh, for real? Oh, okay, that's wuzzup," I said, adjusting myself in the seat as sweat formed on my nose.

Oh, shit. This nigga feelin' me like that, I thought, folding my hands in my lap.

Deion then reached into his console and pulled out a blunt. "You wanna smoke?" he asked.

"Hell yeah," I said.

We rode through the city smoking and vibing.

"So, I know you got hella bitches and shit."

"I ain't gon' lie. I fucks wit' a few, but I ain't got no female living with me or no shit like that."

"I feel you on that."

"What about you? I know yo' fine ass got a nigga," he stated, licking his lip. Deion was different from Tyrell just wit' his approach. He lived by the street code—*kill or be killed*—so he always paid attention to his surroundings. He wasn't the type to put himself in a position to get caught slippin'.

"Naw, we broke up two months ago and shit. I just been chillin'," I said, going into detail about Tyrell.

Deion and I started hanging together heavily every day. We smoked and talked, as he put me up on how to get money and survive. It was something about him that made me want to give him all of me, but I was uneasy about when and how. The closer we got, I knew whatever he had with them other bitches wasn't the same as what we shared.

We were chilling at Deion's for a change instead of going out. My nerves were on high because this was the first time I had been to his house. Things had gotten hot and heavy quickly, and I had no clue how to slow it down.

"Ummm, I need to go to the bathroom."

"Fa sho. It's right down the hall."

"I'll be right back," I said, kissing his lips before getting up. Once I got in the bathroom, I immediately locked the door behind me. My hands were clammy, and my heart was racing. Staring at my reflection in the mirror, I began having a pep talk with myself. "You knew what it was when you decided to come here," I whispered. "Shit," I mumbled as the thought of his touch sent chills across my pussy. This step was serious. If my brothers knew what I was getting ready to do with this nigga, they would beat my ass. Taking a real hard look at myself in the mirror, I had to laugh before walking out of the bathroom as Mary J. Blige's "Real Love" echoed through the apartment.

"Damn, that's my joint right there," I said, making my way back down the hall, swaying my hips back and forth as the music settled my nerves.

Now standing in front of Deion, I allowed my hips to move in a circular motion, waving my hands and snapping my fingers. Deion leaned forward, passing me the Dutch. Grabbing it, I danced and smoked in front of him. Getting up, he moved closer to me, running his fingers through my hair. As we swayed from side to side in a seductive dance, Deion kissed my neck, sending chills through my body. As he removed my shirt, his electrifying touch caused my pussy to jump. He made his way to my breasts and began sucking on one of my nipples. Blowing his warm breath across the top, he then began flicking it with his tongue. My nipples instantly hardened, and my pussy dripped as the heat from his breath caused me to let out a slight moan. That was all he needed to hear. Deion took my left nipple in his mouth and began to suck on it, this time harder, holding my breast with one hand as his other hand gently caressed my body until reaching the button on my jeans.

"Are you sure you're ready, Bella?" he whispered, pull-ing me closer as he touched every magical part of my body.

Am I sure? He is playin' wit' me, I thought, not able to speak.

As I was standing there frozen by the desire to have more of him, he whispered, "Lay down on the bed, Bella," as he unbuttoned my jeans.

I did what he told me. Walking over to the bed, I lay down as Deion positioned himself between my legs. He kissed and sucked on my neck, moving down to my belly, before removing my jeans. I arched my back as my legs opened, inviting him in. Deion slid down my body, allow-ing his tongue to begin exploring my passion box.

"Oh, shit!" I moaned as I felt a tingling sensation erupt. Grabbing his head, I pushed it further into my body as my stomach filled with butterflies, causing me to lose control of every part of my body. My legs started shaking as my juices were overflowing down my leg.

"Aww, yes," I moaned, placing both hands on his head as he ate my pussy like a champ. He looked up, smiling as he finished feasting, kissing my inner thighs before work-ing his way back up. Still positioned between my legs, Deion kissed my lips, then he eased the head of his dick inside of me.

"Oooh, it hurts," I said as Deion gently worked his dick in inch by inch. He was much larger than Tyrell. The pleasure and pain of his thrusts caused my pussy to gush. "Oh," I said, feeling as if I peed on myself.

"Do you want me to stop?" he whispered, continuing to work in and out of me. "It's okay, Bella. I can stop, baby."

"No," I said, squirming from the cold wetness of the sheets.

Moments later, Deion let out a loud groan as his body stiffened for a few seconds.

Da hell? I thought as he pulled out of me.

"Why did you stop?" I asked, confused. This was nothing that I experienced with Tyrell.

"Shit," he said, rolling over and lighting a blunt.

"Did I do something?" I asked, squinting my eyes.

"Nah, you good," he said, removing the partially torn condom from his dick.

"Whatever," I said, jumping up and grabbing my clothes. I headed to the bathroom with fire under my heels. I closed the door and began to wash up before getting dressed.

Oh, he got me fucked up, I thought, dressing as anger took over my mind. "Fuck this nigga," I mumbled, walking out the bathroom, grabbing my purse, and walking out in embarrassment. I was expecting more.

Laying low for the next few weeks, I needed to clear my mind and find out what I wanted in life. I hadn't spoken to Deion since that night. Brandy and Rico had called me, but I did not return their calls. I couldn't believe that I allowed him to get that close to me. Had I learned nothing from the Tyrell and Rain situation?

I need to get my life together, I thought, sitting on the couch, flipping through channels. Momma and Jake were gone for the weekend, and I was relieved. I couldn't take all that drama right now.

After flipping through a few channels, I saw a commercial for Job Corps. I watched different people pop in and out, giving their testimony. One man said something that hit me hard: "It's hard for teenagers to make it these days without an education."

I was so busy running from my problems that I had stopped going to school. "I need to go back to school, and this program is going to help me do that and get a job," I mumbled. Picking up the phone, I called the number and scheduled an appointment with a recruiter. It was time for me to take control of my life.

The next day, the Job Corps recruiter, Mr. Todd, came out to the house and spoke to me. I had never had someone so invested in my future to encourage me to do better. By the end of the conversation, I decided that this was the change I needed, and because I was nineteen, I didn't need Momma's approval.

When Momma and Jake returned, I told her what I had done.

"Bella Marie, I wish you would have talked to me before you did this. But you are grown now. I just don't think going to Job Corps will work," she said with a disappointed look on her face. I focused on Mr. Todd's words, and three weeks later, I was on my way.

Chapter 9

Two Months Later

I had been in Job Corps for two months now, and I was feeling different. I felt like I had a chance to have a real life. I made friends that did not shame me for my choices, but encouraged and cheered me on through the program.

It was almost time for my next class, so I decided to head to breakfast despite not feeling well. I had wanted eggs, toast, and some sausage for breakfast for the last couple of days, and today they were on the menu. *I can't wait to tear this shit up*, I thought, rubbing my hands together, already tasting everything in my mouth as I walked toward the cafeteria.

Once I got my breakfast, I walked toward a table to sit down. My mouth watered as I took a sip of my orange juice. Putting some hot sauce on my eggs, I was prepared to tear into the plate. However, when I got a whiff of the plate, I became nauseous.

"What the fuck? Something must be spoiled," I mumbled. I put my nose in my plate to determine what item was spoiled on my plate, but the smell alone caused me to throw up all over the cafeteria floor. Running over to the garbage can, I felt like I heaved up every meal I'd had for the last week.

"Bella, you okay?" a teacher asked, feeling my head. I was so embarrassed. I knew something was wrong, so I went to the nurse's station.

"Bella, you okay?" Ms. Patty asked when I walked in her office.

"I'm not feeling well. I just threw up eating breakfast," I said as my stomach began to cramp. "I think something may have been spoiled," I whined as tears formed in my eyes from the pain.

"What did you eat?"

"I had a sip of orange juice, and on my plate, I had eggs with hot sauce, some sausage, and toast. I didn't even get a chance to start eating. The smell made my stomach turn."

Ms. Patty gave me the side-eye, then asked, "Really. Bella, when was your last period?"

"Ummm, I don't know. Sometime last month," I replied, confused by her question.

Ms. Patty looked up, then reached in her desk drawer, pulling out a plastic cup. "Here. Pee in this, write your name on the side of the cup, and place it in the cabinet over the toilet. Then come back and lay down."

"Yes, ma'am," I replied, taking the cup and doing as I was told. When I came out of the bathroom, I lay on the bed.

Five minutes later, she returned with a disappointed look on her face. "Bella, you're pregnant," she said, shaking her head.

"What?" I cried, sitting up. "Pregnant," I repeated, placing my hand over my mouth.

"Why did you not wear a condom?" she lectured.

"We did." I sighed.

What the fuck am I going to do now? I thought, knowing they were going to send me home.

"Bella, you need to call home immediately and let your mother know what's going on," she said. "Here. Use my phone so nobody will be in your business." Then she walked out of the office.

"Yes, ma'am," I said in a low tone.

How am I going to explain this to Momma? I thought, hesitating to dial the number. Taking a deep breath, I picked up the phone and dialed.

"Hello, Momma."

"Bella baby, what's going on?"

"Something has happened, and I need to be picked up," I cried without explaining too much.

"I knew this was a mistake. I will be there in the morning," she said, smacking her lips.

"Yes, ma'am." I hung up.

What am I going to do? I thought as I headed to my room to start packing. Ms. Patty and Mr. Manning, the program director, came to my room and asked if I wanted them there when I told her. I declined, and the next day, Momma arrived to pick me up at 10 a.m. It was bittersweet. All of my friends came to help me pack and carry my things out to the car. I never had so many people to care about me and my well-being. Saying our goodbyes, I got in the car and we pulled off.

We were silent for most of the way home, until Momma spoke. Her face was full of concern, but she didn't want to push the issue. "Bella, baby, what's going on? You haven't been the same since I picked you up."

Placing my hands over my face, I started bawling. "Ma, I'm pregnant. That is why you had to pick me up."

"Shhh, it's okay," she said as she rubbed my shoulder. I heard the hurt in her voice, but she still had a calming tone.

She pulled over at the nearest gas station and parked the car. Reaching her arms out, she said, "Come here, baby girl." Her warm hug was what I needed from her at that moment. I hadn't felt her arms around me like that since I was a child. I wanted this moment to last forever.

"It's gonna be okay. Let's go home," she said before putting the car in drive and pulling off.

Once we made it back to the house, she told me to leave everything in the car and just go lay down, which is what I did. Jake was sitting on the couch. I walked right past the living room and into my room, not saying anything to him.

The next day, I was awakened by a loud noise and doors slamming. Clearly Momma and Jake were arguing. I missed most of it, but I could hear their muffled voices vibrating through the walls. I couldn't hear what they were saying. Slowly getting up, I creeped over to crack the door so I could hear.

"Pregnant? Nah, hell no!" Jake yelled.

"What the fuck, Jake? Stop it. What is she supposed to do?" Momma yelled.

"She needs to find that nigga to take care of his own damn kid."

"Jake, she can't take care of no fuckin' baby by herself. She just got kicked out that program."

"I don't care. All I know is the bitch can't stay here, and I mean that. Either she goes, or I go," he yelled.

Moments later, the front door slammed, and the sound of pots and pans started clanging. I couldn't believe this. I was pregnant. I knew she wasn't going to let this nigga put me out. Getting dressed, I walked into the kitchen and sat down at the table. Momma's face was red, and her eyes were puffy from their argument. I folded my hands on top in silence, not wanting to make the situation worse. After the talk we had in the car, I just knew she was going to allow me and the baby to stay. Staring, I waited for her to make eye contact with me, but she never did.

Moments later, she broke her silence. "I'm sorry, Bella. He is not going to let you stay here. I called Sammy, and he said you could come and stay with them," she said as she stumbled over her words. "Your uncle Freddy is on his way to pick you up and take you to their house."

"Ma, you really gon' let him put me out pregnant?" I asked, looking over at her.

Putting her hand on her hips, she said, "Chile, this man is my husband who pays all of the bills."

I smacked my lips "Are you serious, Ma? It's like that?"

"Bella, I didn't tell you to open your legs. I will still help you out as much as I can, but you can't stay here. Jake is not having you staying here," she said, walking out of the kitchen and into her room.

Nineteen and pregnant. I'd be damned if a nigga was just gon' have me out here wit' a baby and he living his best life. I instantly put a plan in place to start looking for Deion. I had to let him know I was pregnant.

I happened to run into his nephew, Rico. I shot him my number and told him to give it to Deion. I had something very important to tell him. It took a couple of days for him to call.

"Shorty, what's good witcha? You wanted to talk, Rico said."

"Yeah, I do. Umm, I just wanted to let you know that I'm pregnant." I spoke softly

"What? When you find out, Bella?" Deion asked.

"After that night we slept together. I decided that I needed to do better with my life, and I enrolled into Job Corps. Later that week, I was gone."

"I wondered what happened to you. I did ask Rico, but he had no clue, and Brandy damn sure ain't tell us shit."

"Yeah, I was trying to get my shit together. I hope you can understand, Deion."

"I get it. You could have told a nigga, though," he said in a displeased tone.

"All I can say is I'm sorry. I don't know what to do since they kicked me out last week," I said.

"All because you're pregnant?"

"Yeah, it's their policy, I guess.

We talked about everything, and by the end of the conversation, we decided that we would make it work somehow. A week later, I moved into his apartment.

Being around Deion more, our relationship seemed to move fast. I realize there were things I wasn't paying attention to about his habits and behaviors.

Chapter 10

Six Months Later

I got a job at Keyon's just around the corner, a little something to keep the financial boat afloat. It might not have been a game-changer, but it made a difference.

Looking over at the clock, I saw that it was five o'clock. *Time to go*, I thought. I couldn't wait to punch out and head home. Usually, Deion would swing and pick me up, but today he was a no-show.

"Where he at?" I muttered impatiently. After a ten-minute wait, I decided not to wait any longer and made my way home. The walk took me about fifteen minutes. Once I reached our small, two-bedroom apartment on Dysinger Road, I spotted Deion's car parked at the corner. Climbing the stairs, I took a moment to ease my tired feet before heading inside.

Walking in, I kicked my shoes off at the door. Deion was sitting on the couch, smoking a blunt and bagging up some product. I plopped down next to him and leaned in for a kiss. Placing the bags on the table, he pulled his blunt out, blowing the smoke in my face before giving me a kiss.

"Dang, nigga." I coughed, watching him continue to work. "You need some help?" I was curious about the process.

"You really wanna help me?" he asked.

"Yeah," I said, pulling my jacket off.

"Ight, Bella," he said, scooping up a portion of the coke and placing it on the scale. "This ounce of coke weighs twenty-eight grams. You see right here," he said, pointing to the scale window. "Look at it. Tell me what you think."

"Humm," I said, putting my fingers to my chin as I began to analyze it from different angles. "It looks snow white with flakes, some crystals. It almost sparkles in the light. But that smell, it's really strong," I said, holding my nose. "What is that, Deion?"

"Petrol." He laughed. "It's a good thing, and it's pure. Now, we are about to cook this shit up, so watch closely. We are about to change its form from a powder base to a solid, to double our money. Go grab the Pyrex out the cupboard, put some water in it, and place it on the stove. Turn that shit up, too. It needs to boil. Also, get the baking soda down."

"Okay," I said, excited about learning so I could help him.

After completing my tasks, I said, "What's next?"

Deion got up and walked over to the kitchen. I watched as he carefully measured out some baking soda. "Okay, Bella, you have to make sure your ratio is correct. Too much baking soda makes the product weak. It needs to be equal or less than the coke. You got it?"

"Got it," I said, repeating after him.

"We want the best product around," he said, mixing the coke with the baking soda.

I looked on as Deion took two playing cards in his hands, which assisted him in making sure it was thoroughly mixed. Walking over to the stove, he dumped it in the Pyrex dish, rotating the pot for about five minutes before removing it from the heat.

"Bella, grab me the ice tray out of the freezer."

"Okay," I said, opening the freezer and grabbing the ice tray. I loosened a couple of ice cubes before handing them to Deion. Place the ice tray back in the freezer, I was ready for my next set of instructions. I looked on as Deion placed each ice cube one at a time into the Pyrex dish as he continued to rotate the pot. He flicked his wrist in a fast, circular motion.

"Turn on the cold water," he said.

"Okay," I said, doing as I was told.

Deion walked over to the sink and sprinkled a little cold water in the pot before lowering the temperature.

The more I watched, the more I was impressed by the process. "Why do you have to sprinkle cold water on it?" I asked,

"You just solidified it."

"Oooh, okay," I said, smiling. "You are something like a chemist." I laughed.

"Naw, I just know how to get this paper, and you will too when I get done teaching you."

Smiling, I watched inquisitively as he turned off the water and walked toward the counter. Grabbing a knife from the strainer, he slowly began to go around the edges of the pot, trying to loosen it up. Deion was focused, as he was trying not to break it. He took his time.

"Bella, grab me some paper towels, placing them on top of each other right here on the counter."

"Okay," I said, turning slightly to his left. I grabbed a few pieces of paper towel and placed them on the counter. As he flipped the Pyrex dish on top of the paper towels, my eyes got big, "Dang, it looks like a big-ass cookie." I laughed

"Now, this is how you cook this shit up, baby. You got this shit, Bella?"

"Yeah, I got it."

"The next one is on you," he said, looking at me with half a smile before leaning in for a kiss.

"No problem." I laughed, rolling my eyes. Deion and I burst into laughter.

"Okay, let's get serious." He decided to show me multiple ways to cook product, starting with the microwave. In the process of teaching me to cook, he started schooling me on all the dope fiends we served. "These niggas run the most game, so you gotta be on point," he stressed.

I had become so obsessed with this shit that I mastered everything he taught me. For the first time, I felt as if I belonged. I officially quit my job and started working with Deion full time. I was all into the game: mind, body, and soul. We ate what we wanted, drove what we liked, and shopped how we desired. Life was good.

The first of the month was coming fast, and money needed to be made. Deion and I had to cop some work, so I decided to bring my homegirl Tiny along to drive because neither of us had a license.

We pulled up to his cousin Reggie's house. He was cool and all, but I hated coming to the trap. The house sat squarely in the middle of the block, and there was a grassy patch that led to a porch with damaged steps. If anything was going down, we would be fucked up.

Deion's phone started vibrating, and he quickly answered it. Now, when I called him, he never seemed to pick up until the fourth ring.

I'ma let his ass hang himself, I thought, giving him the side eye.

"'Sup, Kat? What's the word?"

Looking over at Deion with fire in my eyes, I snapped, "Kat? Who the fuck is Kat?" I sucked my teeth, cocked my head to the side, and folded my arms, waiting for his response.

"Shhh." He motioned, raising his finger as he continued his conversation.

"Nigga, did you just hush me? Da fuck!" I spat, rolling my eyes before getting out of the car and slamming the door. Deion had been receiving more and more calls like this at all hours of the night. I had to walk away before I lost my shit in front of Tiny.

"Let's go, Tiny," I spat as we both got out of the car.

"Bella, what the fuck? You just gon' let that nigga shush you like that? The fuck?" Tiny asked with a confused look on her face.

As we walked the rocky path to the front door, I tried to calm down before answering. "It's business. You know how that shit be, girl," I said, not wanting her to know I was suspicious of his behavior. Once females feel there is a problem, they have too many opinions about what you should do in your relationship.

I tapped on the screen door. A deep voice yelled, "'Sup, Bella ? Come in."

"How y'all doing?" I said as Tiny and I walked into the house. "This my home girl Tiny," I announced.

Moments later, I heard Deion walking up the stairs behind us, talking shit to everyone he saw. Once he was in the house, Deion motioned for us to sit on the gray sectional in the corner. "Ahh, sit here. I'll be right back," he instructed.

"Don't be long, Deion. I mean it," I said, still upset. I watched as he disappeared into the back room with Reggie and the other fellas.

As Tiny and I sat on the couch waiting for Deion, I scanned the living room. The couch sat across from the television stand against a wall. The room was decorated with peeling yellow paint and fly traps that hung from the ceiling. "Shid, we in the only spot that ain't cluttered with junk," I whispered to Tiny.

Tiny giggled, shaking her head. "Gurrrrlll," she replied. "I mean, *who lives like this?*" I said, inspecting the area around me for roaches. The floor was covered with blunt guts, ashes, a few toddler toys, and a ton of empty forty-ounce bottles that were lined up perfectly on the wooden floor. Looking to my left, there was a dining room that had a huge pool table in the middle of the room.

Moments later, Deion, Reggie, and a few other niggas walked out of the back room and were standing around the pool table, talking. He looked over at me. We made eye contact, and I gave him an evil glare to let him know I was ready to go.

Tiny's knee started bouncing as she rubbed her tights. She swooped her long, dark, straight hair behind her left ear and kept looking around at the floor. "Gurl," she said with an anxious look on her face.

"You good? What's wrong?" I asked.

"Bella, I'm good. I feel like them niggas keep longer over here. Maybe I'm trippin'?"

"Hahaha," I started laughing. "I was nervous the first time I came, but we good. They just a bunch of real hood niggas. Here, take this and roll up," I said, trying to distract her.

"Damn, Bella, this looks good. Where did you get this?"

"Right, it does look good, and it smells exquisite. Ain't no telling where Deion got this from. I can ask him, if you want me to," I told her.

"Bet. I can't wait to see how this smoke," she said, licking the end of the Dutch Master.

"I'm a little jealous right now. I wanna hit that too." I laughed. Hearing the screen door slam, I looked over to see Junebug running into the house, sweating and breathing heavily. Junebug was a rougher version of Deion. All he needed was a straight razor the way he was looking, real muscular and solid. Junebug was a gutta-ass nigga from all the bids he had done, but he was always in his bag.

"What up, sis-in-law?" he said, bending down and kissing me on my cheek. "How is my niecey doing?" he asked, rubbing my belly. "Where's D?" he asked, not looking around.

"Shit, right there," I said, pointing toward the dining room. "Can't you tell? She's good. Look how big I am." I smiled.

"Y'all going back home after this?" he asked.

"Yeah, June. What's up?"

"Can I get a ride back with y'all?"

"I don't think that will be a problem. There's enough room," I replied.

We all sat in the living room for about thirty minutes until Deion finally finished handling business, and we headed out.

"Y'all be easy on that ride home," Reggie said, walking us out.

"No doubt, cuz," Deion said, dabbing up Reggie.

"Thanks again," I said as we all headed to get in the car. Deion and I got in the front, while Tiny and Junebug sat in the back. Once inside, I tried to find us something on the radio to ride home to. When Deion's phone vibrated back to back, he didn't answer this time. Looking over at the screen, my blood started to boil.

Who the fuck is Kat? I thought.

Glancing at the side mirror, I began to panic as red and blue lights lit up the highway. As we pulled over, I looked at Deion nervously. My mind and my heart were racing as I tried to keep calm. I had a million questions going through my head. What *are we going to do? Who could I even call? What about my baby?*

Taking in a deep breath, I paused for a second. "Deion, give me the drugs now," I instructed.

"Bella, are you sure?" Deion asked reluctantly.

"Deion," I said, giving him a stern look.

He slid the drugs over to me, and I discreetly placed the drugs in both breasts before pulling up my dress and placing the remainder in my panties.

"I love you, Bella Marie," Deion said.

"I love you too," I replied.

Within moments, the officers were exiting their patrol cars. "Keep calm," I said, looking in the rearview mirror at Tiny, who had a look of panic. I smacked my lips. "Bitch, get it together," I whispered.

With guns raised, the two officers, one black and one white, walked up along each side of the car, pounding on the trunk.

"Turn the fucking car off and hold your hands up, now," the white officer instructed.

Then the black officer walked up to the window. "License and registration."

Looking the officer in his eyes, Deion nodded and slowly reached down into the middle console, pulling out his wallet. He opened it up and handed his permit to the officer through the window that was rolled halfway down.

"Who is the licensed driver?" he asked.

"Me," Tiny said as her voice cracked. Reaching in her pocket, she pulled out her license and handed it to him.

"Sit tight while I check to see if y'all are good," the officer said.

The other cop on my side of the car asked, "Are there any weapons or drugs in the car? I can smell marijuana coming from the inside of the vehic—"

"Why did we get pulled over in the first place, officer?" Deion interrupted.

"Failure to signal," the officer replied. "Are there any guns in the car?" he asked with tension in his voice.

Eight months pregnant with half a brick on my body, I quickly spoke up. "No guns, sir, but I do have this bag of weed," I said, pulling it out of the ashtray and giving it to him.

Taking the bag out of my hand, the officer examined it. He smelled it and said, "It's garbage." He laughed. Dumping the contents of the bag on the ground, the officer instantly squished weed into the concrete with his shoe.

"Get out of the car, all of you."

Complying with the officer, we all got out of the car. Junebug was the first one who they hemmed up.

"Turn around and put your hands behind your back," the white officer said.

"What I do? June blurted out as they cuffed him. Before walking him toward their car, they started his Miranda rights. The further they walked away, I couldn't hear what they were asking him. All I could see was them searching him and throwing him in the back of the police car. Looking over at Deion, I saw the hurt in his eyes. His family meant everything to him, and I respected it. Even though we didn't speak about it, this very moment would change everything.

Fear cascaded through my body as the officer approached me. "Ma'am, I need your identification."

"Okay, it's in my purse in the car," I said, pointing to the front seat of the car.

"I have to handcuff you until we sort this out," the officer said, standing in front of me.

"I am pregnant," I said, causing my voice to echo.

All of a sudden, I heard, "She's pregnant. Be careful wit' her." It was Reggie, yelling and running in our direction.

"Where the hell did he come from?" the white officer spat. "Sir, we have this under control," he shouted as he cuffed my hands in front of me, then guided me to the front seat of our car. "Sit tight, ma'am," he said, patting my shoulder.

"Okay," I said, holding my composure.

They cuffed Tiny and placed her in the backseat of our car, leaving Deion outside, sitting on the curb. As soon as the officer put Tiny in the car and walked away, she had some smart shit to say.

"I'm not going to jail for you or your nigga, Bella," she said with an attitude.

"Tiny, are you serious, bitch? You trying to get us popped?" I whispered as the officer came near the car. Not saying another word, I watched the officer uncuff Deion. Then he came to the car and uncuffed both myself and Tiny.

"You good, Bella?" Deion asked.

"Yes. I'm okay," I replied.

"Y'all good to go, but your homeboy is going to jail. He has outstanding warrants," the officer advised.

"That's my brother. What are his warrants for?" Deion said.

The officer handed Deion a card. "You can call down to the station. He has to be processed first, but they will answer your questions," he said.

Deion nodded his head, acknowledging he understood what to do. "One more thing, officer. Can I see my brother real quick?"

"No," he said, walking away and getting in his car.

Deion walked towards Reggie, who was still on the block, making sure we were good. As I got back into the car, Tiny followed, getting in the back seat. I was not over her little comment, nor the way she tried to play us.

"Aye, Tiny," I said, looking at her through the visor mirror.

"What?" she replied, not even looking up.

"I don't know what type of bullshit you tried pulling, but that shit ain't cute. You better be thankful I am pregnant," I said, pushing the visor up.

"You're mad because I wasn't about to take a charge for y'all?" she snapped.

"Bitch, you know damn well you weren't taking no charge for nobody," I spat. "Matter of fact, bitch," I said, getting out of the car and opening the back passenger door. "Get the fuck out," I yelled, boldly pointing my finger at her forehead.

Tiny didn't move or reply.

Deion walked up to the car. "Bella, get back in the car and shut the fuck up," he yelled. "Yo, this shit can wait. You trippin'," he said, getting into the car.

I followed suit, but I was still pissed. *I can't believe this bitch. I want to kick her ass,* I thought. Looking over at Deion, I placed my hand on his thigh as we rode silently back to Lockport.

Once we hit the city limit, Tiny said, "Deion, can you drop me off at the house?"

"Yeah, I gotchu," Deion said.

"Can you just hurry? I have to go to the bathroom," I said as a crease formed across my forehead. "This bitch," I mumbled.

Twenty minutes later, we pulled up to Tiny's house. I was excited. That meant I was one step closer to the crib and cutting this bitch off.

Opening the back door, she grabbed her purse and began getting out of the car. "All right now. Thanks, y'all," she said before stepping out and closing the door behind her.

"Bitch, please," I barked out.

"Stop it, Bella. Some shit you just gotta let slide."

"Don't do that! Deion, you know she was deadass wrong," I said as he pulled off. That quick little trip to the crib felt like forever. I couldn't help but to wonder why Deion wasn't mad too.

Once we pulled up to the house, I got out and went straight in the house and into the bathroom. Pulling the drugs from my bra and my panties and placing them on the bathroom sink, I could hear Deion talking.

Opening the door, I yelled, "You talking to me, Deion?"

"Naw," Deion replied, continuing his call.

Finishing up in the bathroom, I grabbed the drugs off the sink and went into the living room. Placing the drugs on the coffee table, I stood in the middle of the floor, observing Deion in the kitchen, opening a package that was left at the door. "D...Deion? Who sent that?" I whispered, trying to get his attention, but he waved me off and continued his call.

"Whatever," I mumbled, walking off and into the bedroom to get ready for bed. After everything that happened earlier, I was tired. Grabbing my pajamas, I turned the light off and got straight in the bed. My mind was so heavy. *Who was he talking to, and what was in the package he was opening?* I thought as I drifted off to sleep.

Over the next few weeks, we hustled hard, navigating the streets with precision. Deion and I had just returned from trapping in the Falls. The challenges with the fiends out there were different. Upon entering the house, I took a shower, changed into my pajamas, and turned on the TV. Deion was already on the bed, rolling a Dutch. A smile crept across my face, savoring a moment of quality time with my man—no phone calls, no company. However, Deion's phone vibrated, prompting him to pick it up and start texting. A scowl formed on his face, and I let out a heavy sigh.

"Wuzzup, babe? Who is that?" I asked.

"Kat," he whispered as he engaged intensely with her via text.

"Deion, who the fuck is Kat?"

"Bella, stop trippin'! Just go in the kitchen and make something to eat."

Sucking my teeth, I rolled my eyes, throwing the covers off of me, then headed to make him something to eat. *Dis nigga got me fucked up*, I thought, grabbing a pizza out of the freezer. Removing it from the box, I threw the box on the counter and put the pizza in the oven. I headed into the living room to watch television as I waited for the pizza to cook. Moments later, Deion walked in and plopped his ass down on the couch next to me, placing his phone face down on the table.

"So, you gon' tell me who the fuck Kat is?" I said, throwing my hands up.

"Stop trippin'. It's business."

"Then tell me who she is and how you met her. Because last I checked, we was business partners, so you shouldn't be doing business with nobody I don't know," I said, cocking my head to the side as I awaited an answer.

Deion still had no response.

"Okay," I said before getting back up to check on the pizza. Leaning against the counter with my arms folded, I instantly felt a gush of warm water running down my leg.

"What the fuck? Deion!" I yelled, gripping the counter as pain hit me.

"What's wrong, baby?" he said, rushing into the kitchen.

"Ahhhh! What the fuck!" I yelled as a sharp pain shot up the side of my stomach, causing me to double over. Cradling my stomach, I cried, "Fuck! Dial nine one one,

Deion." Just then, my knees buckled, and I collapsed onto the floor, folding in a fetal position as tears streamed down my eyes. The room began to spin, and I could feel myself about to nod out. I faintly heard Deion saying something to me, but I could not make out the words as I continued to drift in and out. "I. Need—" were my only words before everything faded black.

I was awakened again by a female voice and slight nudge, not sure how long I had been out.

"Bella. Bella. Can you hear me?" she said, shaking me.

"Where are we?" I replied, my mind very cloudy. Just then, another pain shot through my stomach, this time under my belly button, followed by a prick in my arm. Immediately, I beginning to shiver. "What is—"

"Bella, I'll be taking your vitals, okay? Just relax. I just put your IV in. Okay, hon?" she said, covering me with a thin blanket.

"I don't give a fuck," I whispered as my teeth began to chatter. Everything was surreal. Chills came over me. Placing a hand on my belly, I whispered, "Please, Lord, not my baby. Lord, please." Tears streamed down my cheeks as I began to say a silent prayer.

When we got to the hospital, it seemed like forever for them to get me upstairs. As the nurse hooked me up to the machine, I grabbed her hand and cried, "Check my daughter's heartbeat."

"Your daughter has a heartbeat and is fine. It was checked in the ambulance. Now please, relax," she said in a calming voice, patting my hand.

"Please check again. Something is wrong. Something feels wrong," I pleaded.

"Okay," she said, rechecking the baby's vitals. She ran the strip of paper through her hands, and she said, "I'm going to get the doctor. You rest." A flushed look came over her face.

Deion looked over at me and smiled. "Bella, baby, just relax everything will be okay." He leaned over to hold me.

Moments later, the doctor walked in and introduced himself. "Greetings, Bella, I am doctor Shabaze." He smiled and started looking over my chart.

"How is my baby?" I cried, wanting him to cut the small talk.

Looking me in the eyes, he said in a gentle voice, "I am so very sorry, but your baby has no heartbeat. I'm going to give you a moment, and then we will need to prep you for a D&C." He walked out of the room.

I couldn't move. "Why? Why . . . us, Lord?" I cried, knowing my baby Deja was gone.

"It's going to be okay," he said as a single tear dropped out of the corner of his eye. Squeezing my hand, Deion said, "We will get through this. I promise."

"How, Deion? Tell me, please," I snapped, then turned on my side as tears fell.

"I'm sorry, I'm sorry. Bella, I'm tryin'," he said.

Watching Deion, I saw his tears begin to fall, but I felt no sympathy for him.

"Knock, knock. It's your nurse, Ms. Goins," she said, walking in. "I'm Nurse Jackson. I'm here to prep you. Do you have any questions, honey?"

I didn't respond as she began to prep me. "We gon' put you on your back, sweetie. I have put medicine in your IV that will make you sleepy. Doctor Shabaze wants you to rest a bit."

I didn't sleep much after the medicine. I was in pain from the contractions that came back to back. Within the next six hours, I would deliver a stillborn.

Chapter 11

Watching the neighborhood kids playing outside through the window brought joy and pain to my heart. I was still struggling with the loss of my baby girl, and grief had definitely etched its mask on my soul. Something inside me was lost. That miscarriage killed a radiant spark that I could not seem to get back.

Placing my hand on my belly, I whispered, "Deja." My relationship with Deion was seemingly hanging on by a thread as we both struggled with the loss in our own way. Our love that once seemed so strong was fading by the day, but our commitment to one another was the bond that held us together. I wanted to start my family and have something to hold onto forever, but in the game, having a family can be a liability.

Deion walked into the living room. The silence between us echoed with so much pain and words not spoken. Over the last few months, he had tried to get us back on track. I just hadn't been able to receive him.

We started trapping again, but this time it was on a whole new level. The cash flow now? It made our previous endeavors look like spare change. We moved with a confidence that silenced any doubt, playing our cards discreetly and keeping a low profile with every move. We were living the good life as we died slowly to grief. I believe that God makes no mistakes, and the struggles we faced had become stepping stones to this moment, where nobody could question our hustle.

"I'm 'bout to make this quick run, but let's hit the club tonight," he said, grabbing his keys off the coffee table.

"Okay, coo'," I replied as I continued to stare out the window.

"Ight, be ready about eight," he said, walking out the door.

Without replying, I just continued to watch the children in the neighborhood play.

Later that evening, Deion suggested we head to The Ballroom in Buffalo. It struck me as odd, since Buffalo wasn't our usual hangout, but apparently, it had become the newest hot spot. My curiosity was piqued, so I agreed to check it out and see what the buzz was all about.

When we walked in the bar, a faint smell of YSL was intercepted by my nose. Everybody who was anybody in the streets was there that night, because it was jumpin'.

We sat at a table off to the side of the bar, and Jeezy blazed through the club. Bopping my head and snapping my fingers, I loosened up as the music took my soul to a new level. "Oh, this my jam," I said, waving my hand.

"I'm 'bout to get us some shots." He leaned over and spoke in my ear.

Turning up my lip, I shook my head no. Deion leaned back in and said, "What the fuck, Bella? You gotta loosen up. Come on."

"Okay, just one," I said, leaning over in his ear as I let out a heavy sigh. Drinking had never been my thing, but he was right. I did need to loosen up.

He nodded his head and got up to head over to the bar.

I wonder how he heard of this place, I thought, continuing to vibe off the music.

Looking over at the bar, I noticed he was really friendly with the bartender, but I paid it no mind. Moments later, he returned with two double shots of Hennessy for each of us and a beer. He placed the glasses in the middle of the table and his beer in front of himself. I rolled my eyes at a smiling Deion, grabbing one of the shot glasses and throwing back the Hennessy.

"Wheeeeewwwwwww!" I shouted, slamming the glass down on the table. The liquor went down hot and hard as I looked over at Deion, who had already took both his shots and was now sipping on his beer. He pointed to the second glass, gesturing for me to drink it. Grabbing the second shot glass, I threw back the last shot of Hennessy.

"Wheeeeewwwwwww!" I shouted, slamming the second glass down on the table. After the second shot, I started getting hot and feeling dizzy. Getting up, I took off my jacket, throwing it on my chair as I started grinding in Deion's lap. I was feeling good. The clinking of glasses and murmur of conversations created a nostalgia like never before. It had been a while since I felt this alive.

As the night unfolded, our conversation took on a rhythm of its own, alternating between heartfelt confessions and playful banter. Placing my hands on Deion's knees, I dipped down low, working my hips left and right on the way up. Just then, the bartender approached us with four more shots and a beer for Deion.

She leaned over and whispered in Deion's ear before placing the drinks on the table. I paused, instantly giving her an ice cold glare before she walked away.

Pulling me down in his lap, he said. "Stop it. She was only telling me it was on the house."

"I'm ready to go," I leaned back and whispered in his ear, pulling myself off his lap. I started putting on my coat.

Deion didn't argue with me. He got up, pulling a fifty-dollar bill out of his pocket and placing it on the table. Looking me up and down, he grabbed my hand and led me out of the club to our truck. Once we got to the truck, he opened my door. I climbed in, pulling my coat off and throwing it on the back seat. Deion got in the truck, started it up, and we pulled off.

Leaning over the middle console, I unzipped Deion's jeans, pulling his dick out. Spitting on the tip, I used my tongue to slurp it back up.

"Oh, shhh . . . You know what a nigga like," he said. "Hell yeah," he moaned as I started gagging and raising my head back up as Jeezy blazed through the speakers. "Shhhhh," he said, pulling over into an empty parking lot.

Bobbing my head up and down to the beat, I tried to suck the soul out of his body. Once done, I sat up and placed my feet on the dashboard, looking over at Deion as he pulled back off. I licked two fingers as he watched me pleasuring myself until we pulled up to the house.

Walking in the door, our clothes came flying off as we went up the stairs. "Bend over the railing, Bella," he instructed.

"Yess, daddy," I replied, allowing my panties to fall to my ankles. He spread my legs apart, eating my pussy from behind.

"Yess, baby," I moaned. "Eat this shit." I reached my arm back, gripping the back of his head.

Raising his head just a little as his hands separated my cheeks, Deion began to eat my ass.

"Oh, yes, baby!" I yelled as my body began to tremble. My juices started squirting on his face.

Deion picked me up, leaning my back slightly against the wall, tightly wrapping my legs around his waist. This shit was intense. I felt every bit of his ten inches inside. "Awww, aww, yes, daddy. Fuck your pussy," I yelled.

Deion hugged me a little tighter as he walked to the couch and sat down, still holding me close. Hopping off of him, I got on my knees and started sucking and licking all my juices off his dick. I played with his balls as I looked at him. His eyes closed as his head was leaning back.

"Yess, Bella," he moaned as his body began to twitch. I knew he was getting ready to explode. I lifted my head as he towered over me. Grabbing my ponytail, he pulled my head back as he started jacking off.

"Is this what you want?" he said, staring me in my eyes.

"Yes, daddy," I whispered just as he bust all in my face.

Using my shirt to wipe my face, Deion whispered, "Meet me in the bedroom."

"Okay, let me go to the bathroom real quick." As I headed to the bathroom, I heard his phone ring. I stood at the edge of the door, eavesdropping for a moment.

"What's good, Kat? Naw, everything is straight. What time?" he said in a low tone.

Just then, I walked back in, glaring at Deion with fire in my eyes. "Who the fuck is Kat, and why is she calling at this hour? Where you think you going, nigga?"

"You always do the most, Bella. I thought you were going to the bathroom."

"Fuck that, nigga. Are you fucking this bitch?"

"I told you it's business. I got some shit lined up with her and her boss."

Storming off to the bathroom, I slammed the door behind me.

Knock knock knock.

"Bella, why you trippin on me?"

"Deion, what the fuck are we doin'? Do you even wanna be here?"

"It's not like that, baby. I met a new connect when I took a ride to the Bronx. I think we can get what we need at a cheaper cost working with them. I didn't want to say anything yet, but we will need to meet with them."

I smacked my lips as I leaned against the door. "Whatever, nigga. You've been real sneaky lately."

"Open the door, Bella," he asked.

Not responding, I waited a second before opening the door. I looked at him.

"Trust me, baby, I got us." Grabbing my hand, he led us back out of the bathroom.

The next morning, the sunlight filtering through the curtains gently woke me from a peaceful sleep. As I reached for my phone on the nightstand, the screen lit up with an incoming call from Deion's cousin Nikki. I answered with a groggy voice.

"Hey, girl."

"Hey, girl! How you doing?" Nikki's warm voice resonated through the phone.

I stretched and sat up, rubbing the sleep from my eyes. "I'm good. What's up?"

There was a moment of hesitation on the other end before Nikki sighed. "I need to talk to you about something. Can I come over?" Concern laced her words, and I could sense that something important weighed on her mind.

"Of course," I said before we ended our call. I quickly got ready, my mind buzzing with curiosity. As I headed downstairs to make us something to eat, I couldn't shake the feeling that this conversation held significance.

About an hour later, Nikki walked in the house and greeted me with a warm hug, her burgundy hair catching the sunlight as she sat at the kitchen table. "I know you love my fried chicken, so I hooked you up, sis." I smiled as we settled at the table to eat. Nikki's eyes met mine, and a mix of emotions were in her eyes.

"I wanted to talk to you because . . . well, I'm pregnant," she revealed, her eyes searching for my reaction.

"Oh my God, girl," I cried, overflowing with happiness for her. "Nikki, that's amazing news! Congratulations!"

Tension released from Nikki's shoulders as she grinned back. "Thank you, girl. But there's more. I know you and Deion don't always see eye to eye, but I trust you. I want you to be a part of my baby's life, and I hope we can put any differences aside for the sake of family."

"Absolutely, Nikki. I'll be here for you every step of the way."

Deion's family and I had weathered our share of issues, but in that moment, I knew that Nikki and I had forged a bond. Sometimes, life takes unexpected turns to bring people closer, and I was grateful for the unexpected friendship that had blossomed between us.

Chapter 12

The positive pregnancy test in my hands brought a flood of emotions. I could hardly believe that I was going to be a mother again, and this time, it felt like a second chance, a fresh start. Determined to create a different life for this child, I made a silent vow to break free from the shadows of the past. As the news settled in, I knew I needed to make changes, not just for myself, but for our growing family. I had to protect this baby from the life we lived. The decision to find a real job was made, but I continued to support Deion, standing by his side through thick and thin.

I noticed the pressure from his family and the conflict of hustling began taking a toll on him. *I wonder if bringing a child into our current situation is the right move*, I thought, placing my hands over my belly.

Deion was in the bedroom counting money. I hesitated walking in and just stood by the doorway, watching. My stomach was turning cartwheels, and a feeling of vulnerability and hope sent chills up my spine. I had another chance to be a mother. Taking a deep breath, I was nervously fidgeting with my hair at the unknown action from Deion.

"Babe," I said in a soft, steady voice. "There is something that I need to tell you." I walked into the room and siat on the bed next to him.

Deion wrapped the stack of money in a rubber band, looking up as if he sensed something going on. He set the money aside, giving me his full attention. "Wuzzup, Bella?"

As I began to speak, my words carried the weight of an unspoken history. "I took a pregnancy test today, and I'm pregnant, Deion."

There was a moment of silence, then his eyes got big with excitement. Pausing for a moment, his expression changed as concern painted his face. "Pregnant."

I nodded my head as my eyes dropped to the floor. "Yes," I whispered. "Look, I know I have been different since we lost Deja, but God has given us a chance to do it again. We have to make better choices now that we are having a baby."

The air in the room was stiff as Deion processed the weight of my words. He nodded his head and reached for my hand. "Bella, whatever I gotta do for us, you know I will do."

Tears welled up in my eyes as I spoke. "Our chance is now."

Deion pulled me into him. The silence between us spoke volumes. At this moment, I knew it was time for a new beginning.

"I'm here for our family, Bella," Deion whispered, placing a kiss on my forehead. "No matter what we face, we will face it together," he said, holding me tight.

As I was in his arms, the weight of our journey and the promise of a future created a healing space in that moment.

We had been trapping out of our apartment for a minute, and it was now time for us to move and leave the hustle behind. Our journey led us to Lowertown about three months later, a place where we hoped to build a stable and secure life for our growing family. Deion landed a job at the Best Western, taking on the role of a janitor, while I started making coffee at Tim Hortons. Working legal jobs side by side felt like a fresh start, a chance to redefine our lives and prioritize our family legally. We faced our struggles head-on, navigating through the challenges of our new life in Lowertown.

Over the next five months, through hard work and resilience, we began to see the fruits of our labor. The stability we craved started to materialize, and despite the odds, we were making things happen. Our journey was far from easy, but with each passing day, we were building a foundation that would provide a brighter future for our family—one that was rooted in love, stability, and the shared commitment to a life beyond the shadows of our past.

But dealing with his family had become more difficult after we moved.

Nikki came over to the house to help me prepare the baby's room. We had gotten super close over time, so much so that the family started turning on her, too. But she was there for me every step of the way, especially with my fears of dealing with this pregnancy. Nikki had just had her baby, but she knew I was extremely nervous because of what happened to my first child.

We had finished the room, and she was headed to pick her kids up from school. "You call me if you need anything, Bella."

The doctors had tried to reassure me that everything looked good, but I still couldn't believe them until my baby was in my arms. Preparing to meet our young king in the making, I washed and folded the last of Junior.'s clothes. After putting the last item away, I got a sharp pain in my back, and fear took over my body.

"Deion!" I yelled, gripping onto the dresser.

Moments later, he was by my side with panic in his eyes. "Bella, babe," he yelled, trying to help me to the bed.

"I think we need to go to the hospital. My bag is in the closet," I said as the pain intensified.

He grabbed the bag from the closet and helped me to the car. Twenty minutes later, we pulled up to the hospital. Giving him an intense glare, I could tell that Deion was high as fuck.

"Deion, I'm scared."

"Me too, but I know everything will be all right this time, Bella," he said, grabbing the bag and helping me out of the car.

Entering through the doors, the nurse swiftly guided me upstairs to the maternity ward and settled me into my room in no time. Despite the excitement of the moment, there was a tinge of disappointment, knowing it could have been even more special if my mom had made it to the hospital.

Deion immediately began rubbing my back. "I promise I'll make sure you're good," he assured, sealing his words with a gentle kiss on my forehead.

"Thank you," I said as the pain reflected on my face.

After enduring twenty hours of labor, Deion Jermaine Jackson came into the world—eight pounds, eight ounces, and twenty-nine inches long. In that moment, life stood still, and nothing else mattered except my newborn. Despite the pain and tears, I made a solemn promise to myself that I wouldn't go through this again for a long time.

The next day, my mom and Deion's mom came to the hospital. What was meant to be a joyous moment quickly went left when my mom looked over at the baby and said, "He may look like y'all, but at least he has our color."

"Mom!" I shouted out, feeling a wave of embarrassment wash over me as Deion and his mother exited the room. If we had the ability to choose our parents, I was wishing for a different life at this moment.

Months had passed since the baby and I were released from the hospital, and things between Deion and me took a turn for the worse. A growing disconnect loomed. Every attempt I made to communicate resulted in heated arguments. It was like talking to a brick wall. As our finances dwindled and the pressure set in, I reached a breaking point. I couldn't endure it any longer. Living on a standard income wasn't enough. Unemployed at the time, I felt the only solution was to return to the hustle to make ends meet. I just needed to find a way to convince Deion.

Following dinner, I opted to put the baby to bed early, intending to create an intimate atmosphere for an important conversation. Entering the shower, I stood in contemplation as the water enveloped me. I pondered how to broach the upcoming discussion casually. After thirty minutes, I emerged from the shower, wrapping myself in a towel. Applying lotion to my body, I selected something enticing in his preferred color.

Swiftly, I donned a sexy garment that perfectly complemented my figure, adding a touch of allure to the ambiance. The white Chanel teddy perfectly cuffed my perky double D breasts. Giving them a shake, I admired my body in the mirror, and my pussy moistened as the thought of riding Deion's dick ran through my mind. Misting myself with Intrusion perfume added that extra touch, just how he liked it. Walking over to my closet, I put on my red heels. I took one last glance in the mirror before heading back downstairs.

"You is a pretty bitch," I mumbled, feeling on point.

Walking down the steps slowly, I let my fingers graze the railing as one foot crossed the other, popping my hips from left to right. When I got downstairs, Deion was sitting on the couch, smoking a Dutch and watching Monday night football.

"You want a beer, babe?" I asked, trying to get his attention.

"Yeah," he said, never looking up.

Smacking my lips in mild irritation, I rolled my eyes while entering the kitchen. Opening the refrigerator, I swiftly grabbed a beer for him and a water for myself before shutting it. Gathering my composure, I adjusted my teddy and returned to the living room. Seating myself beside Deion, I handed him his beer. He passed the weed, a smile playing on his lips as he appreciatively scanned me from head to toe.

"Wuzzup? You lookin' real good over dere."

I smiled, tasting the seduction on my lip. "Nuttin'," I said, exuding a hint of sass as I hit the weed a couple of times then climbed on his lap. "Open your mouth," I said before taking another long pull, then blowing the smoke into Deion's mouth. I sucked on his bottom lip. Pulling back, I hit the weed again before passing it to him. I started kissing his neck.

Working my way to his ear, I whispered, "Fuck me right here." I swayed my hips back and forth in slow motion. As I rubbed my pierced nipples against his chest, Deion smacked my ass. Lifting slightly, he undid his jeans and pulled his rock-hard dick out. I sighed as I slid down on all ten inches. Deion grabbed my waist as I began to ride him. I could feel he wanted me just as much as I wanted him.

"Bitch, is this my pussy?" Deion asked, grabbing my neck.

"Yess! Yes, baby." Instantly I got even wetter as I tightened my grip around his dick.

Pulling my hair as he sucked on one of my breasts, he busted inside of me. Coming down from our sexual high, I embraced him. Using this time, I put my plan in motion and dropped the seed in his ear about trappin'. I might have been wrong playing on his weakness, but we needed to get back in the game.

A few weeks later, Deion was back on his grind, and tension filled the air. He had to head to the Bronx to see Kat, accompanied by his nephew, Rico. This was meant to be a quick turnaround. I stayed home with the baby because he had a little cold.

When Deion finally checked in around noon, relief washed over me.

"Wuzzup?"

"You good, babe?"

"Yeah, everything checks out."

"Okay, when are you leaving?"

"Shit, we about to leave now."

"Okay, I love you," I said, hanging up. The nervousness of that ride always lingered in the background.

While waiting for their return. I was chilling in the living room, anticipating his safe homecoming. Looking at my phone, I saw ten missed calls, all from Deion. I realized my phone was on silent. Panicking, I called him back immediately.

"Baby, what the fuck is goin' on?"

"Bella, you are not going to believe this shit."

"What happened, Deion?"

He explained that they stopped in Clarendon at the Circle K for gas and a drink, a move we rarely made due to the area's known racism.

"Nephew started to go in on this ho as we about to pump this gas and head back."

"Yeah, get the fuck up outta there."

Suddenly, I heard a woman yelling in the background, signaling trouble.

"Fuck that white bitch, nephew. Let's go," he yelled as we continued talking. Suddenly, Deion sighed heavily.

A half hour later. Deion yelled, "Oh, shit, Bella! They pulling us over."

"Pulled y'all over? Are you serious, Deion?" I yelled, hearing Deion say, "Nephew, throw the dope out the window while we still have a chance."

"Unc, fuck that. I got us," Rico said in the background.

"Fuck, why can't he listen?" I shouted, frustrated that Deion's nephew was not cooperating. All of a sudden, I heard them arguing in the background.

"Nigga, they don't have a reason to search us. We good, Unc."

I knew Rico's bullheadedness was at play, and hearing the frustration in Deion's voice left me uneasy. "Why the fuck you don't listen to me, nigga?" he yelled.

Just then, I heard an officer demanding license and registration.

"No, call a white shirt," Rico said in an aggressive tone, which escalated the situation.

"Boy, step out of the vehicle now with your hands up," the officer yelled, and the phone disconnected, leaving me in shock.

"Fuck! I just can't believe this shit!" I yelled, pacing the floor. "What in the hell is Kitty going to say when she finds out? What the fuck did I get us into?" I snapped as panic took over my mind. Kitty was Rico's mom and Deion's older sister. She was someone I respected for always keeping me informed. Letting her know about this ordeal wouldn't be easy.

***

Four hours later, Deion came into the house, slamming the door behind him. He walked to the kitchen where I was cooking dinner. Leaning over the counter, he took his hat off and rubbed his forehead. The look on his face frightened me. I hadn't seen that look on his face since Junebug got arrested. I waited patiently for Deion to speak to me first as I turned off the stove.

"Roll up," he said in a somber tone as he told me what happened.

I listened intently before asking, "So, how Rico slip the dope under his seat? Did he not believe they would search the car?"

"I don't know, Bella. All I know is he took that charge for me, babe," Deion said. "Why didn't he just listen?" Deion said as his voice began to crack.

Walking over to him, I lifted his head. "We got this. I have your back. I love you, baby," I told him before leaning in to kiss him.

Deion had one more thing to do before the end of the night. He had to call Kitty to let her know the situation. I couldn't bear to listen to the conversation, so I headed to check on Junior.

All that night, I tossed and turned in my sleep. I don't think I slept a wink. My nerves were so bad. I knew it was about to go down.

The following day, I heard a loud banging on the back door. I ran into Junior's room to look out the window. "Shit," I yelled as I saw all three of Deion's sisters standing outside. "I'm coming!" I shouted out the window.

I rushed into our room to wake up Deion, who was already sitting on the edge of the bed, throwing his shorts on, mumbling as he rubbed his eyes. He stood up and headed downstairs to let them in.

I could hear them talking calmly at first, but that escalated quickly. All three of Deion's sisters went the fuck off on him.

Peeking around the railing, I saw Kitty, lipstick smeared as the tears rolled down her cheeks. As Deion explained more, she started screaming Jehovah's name.

His sister Amy was so pissed. She walked out of the house, still fussing as the other two followed her.

I finally came downstairs when the coast was clear. I could still feel the tension in the air. That shit was so thick you could cut it with a knife. As soon as my foot hit the last step, that nigga cut his eyes at me, looking straight through my soul. I could tell his wheels were turning, and I didn't dare ask him what he was thinking. A few moments later, Deion got up and left.

Picking up my phone, I called Nikki. "Girl, can you come to the house? I need to talk to you."

Chapter 13

Deion seemed consumed by the hustle, and I could sense the weight of his misery. The past few weeks had turned him into someone I could barely deal with. It was clear he was tormented by Rico's arrest. Our days became a constant cycle of arguments from sunrise to bedtime. The tension escalated to the point where management gave us an eviction notice. Doubts crept in, and I began to question if this relationship was a mistake. Despite my love for Deion, the strain became unbearable. Something had to change.

We ended up relocating to a place on Olcott Street, and the next few weeks seemed smoother, although I still grappled with the uncertainty of our relationship. Seeking a momentary reprieve, I reached out to Nikki, asking if she could take care of Junior for a few days.

Entering the living room, I found Deion on the couch, rolling up. Sitting down beside him, I could feel the nervous energy lingering between us. Gathering my words, I took a deep breath, crossed my legs, and opened up about what was on my mind.

"Listen, I think we should take a short trip, just you and me. I already spoke to Nikki, and she'll keep Junior while we're gone."

"Great minds think alike."

"What do you mean?"

"I felt we needed a break from the bullshit as well. How does West Palm Beach sound?"

"Okay, bae. I'll book our flights."

"Make sure we're there by Thursday."

"Thursday? Why Thursday?" I questioned, giving him a puzzled look.

"No reason."

"Okay . . . whatever," I said, shaking my head. I went upstairs to start checking flights. Picking the most expensive bundle I could find, I went to the top of the stairs and yelled down, "Deion, how does next Wednesday afternoon sound? We leave at ten forty-five because we have to be there two hours early."

"That's coo'," he replied. "Did you get a rental too?"

"Yeah, it was a package deal."

"A'ight."

The week seemed to go by fast. I did all of the shopping for the trip and packing the day before, so I was ready to go bright and early. I put the finishing touches on my makeup and headed downstairs.

"Deion, take these suitcases to the car," I instructed, making sure I didn't forget anything at the last minute.

"What the fuck you got in here?"

"Nigga, don't do me. Just put the shit in the car, please. I will lock up," I said as I started checking the windows and doors before heading to the car.

Pulling up to the Buffalo Airport, we parked the car and headed into the terminal to check in. Once we got our tickets and made it through security, we finally headed toward the gate.

"You want something to drink or any food, Bella?"

"Naw, I'm good. I'm ready to get on this plane, though," I laughed.

"You ain't never lied."

"Welcome to the sunshine state of Florida," the captain said over the speaker. It was a perfect afternoon. We had arrived, and I could finally breathe. It was time to start our vacation.

Once we made it off the plane, we grabbed our luggage and headed to get the rental. I waited as Deion got the keys, and the man pulled the car out front. I got in the passenger seat, and the guy helped Deion load the luggage in the vehicle. Pulling off, I set the navigation system to the Hilton Garden Inn.

As we got closer to the hotel, Deion's phone was blowing up. "Who's calling you?" I asked, giving him an intense glare.

"Nobody important."

"They are if they calling back-to-back, nigga."

When we arrived at the hotel, I checked in as Deion got our luggage. Once we got in the room, I jumped in the shower. Just as I turned the water on, I heard Deion yell. "Yo, I'll be right back."

Not responding, I rolled my eyes and continued showering. *What the fuck is he up to?* I thought as the hot water flowed over my body. After getting out of the shower, feeling refreshed, it was time to hit the streets.

Walking out of the bathroom, I noticed Deion had not made it back to the room. *Where the fuck is he?*

"This nigga got me fucked up," I spat as I got dressed. Picking up my phone off the dresser, I called him and got no answer. Hitting his line again, there was still no response. I grabbed my purse and headed out the door just as Deion was coming in.

"Why the fuck you ain't answer? And where did you go?"

"Chill with that shit. Let me jump in the shower real quick. We got somewhere to be."

"Where?"

"I gotta handle some shit, and then we can do whatever you want."

"Yeah, a'ight. I'm hungry, so I hope we are going to eat," I said, watching Deion head to the bathroom.

Ten minutes later, Deion was ready.

"'Bout time. Where we goin'," I asked, rolling my eyes.

"To dinner at Hullabaloo for a quick meeting."

"Meeting? Nigga, I thought you said this was a get-away?"

"It is, but something came up that needs to be handled."

"Whatever," I said as we headed to the car. I was missing Junior already, so I shot Nikki a text to let her know we made it safe before putting my phone back in my purse.

Still trying to get in the groove of things, I was pissed that he made business plans during our time.

Deion started making conversation as we made our way to the restaurant. "Listen, I know I said it was just us. After that shit with Rico, this was a meeting that I could not say no to."

"Well, we need to change some shit, because this is not working. We are supposed to be a team, but I seem to be on a need-to-know basis."

"Chill, Bella."

"Chill? Deion, you talk at me instead of talking to me. I never seem to know what's going on until after some shit jumps off."

"I feel you, Bella. I guess with everything going on, I haven't been myself. I'm trying to make sure we get back on track, and I need to get Rico a good lawyer."

"I know you have. Had I never asked you to get back in, then he wouldn't be in jail now."

"Naw, I'm a grown man, and so is Rico. The shit was already on my mind. When you brought it up, all that did was give me confirmation."

"Whatever . . ."

We pulled up to the restaurant as I glanced in the mirror, making sure I was on point. The valet took our keys as Deion and I walked into the restaurant.

"Our party is already seated and expecting us," he told the hostess.

"Yes, Mr. Johnson, this way. Mr. Ramirez is waiting. Follow me," she said, guiding us to the table. As we approached, a distinguished Mexican gentleman and a mixed female stood up. The man reached out to shake our hands, followed by the female.

"Kat," she said, smiling. "It's so nice to meet you, Bella, finally."

"Please, have a seat," Hector instructed. "I've heard good things about you, Bella. Deion, it's unfortunate about your nephew. I hope you have control over everything," he said, taking a drink of the dark liquor in his glass.

"Yes, everything is on track, Mr. Ramirez," Deion said, rubbing his hands together.

Hector glanced over at me as if he was reading my body language. "Bella, what's your poison?" he asked with a smirk on his face.

"I'll take a Crown Royal on the rocks. Make that a double."

"My kind of girl. Deion?" Hector asked, looking in his direction.

"Hennessy on ice will work for me."

"I will have another glass of wine," Kat interjected before Hector waved off the waitress.

"Now, shall we get down to business? That little shakeup has me a little uneasy about your abilities," he said once the waitress was far enough away from the table.

While they discussed the Rico situation, Kat and I became more acquainted. "You look familiar, like I have seen you someplace before," I said.

"I get that a lot, but no, I don't believe we ever met."

"Huh," I said, looking at Deion with fire in my eyes. *So, this bitch gon' lie to my face*, I thought, ready to go off on Deion.

A few moments later, the waitress came back with our drinks. "Are you ready to order, or do you need a few more minutes?"

"We're ready," Hector said, beginning to order.

After placing our orders, the waitress left again, and Deion and Hector continued talking. Hector's following statement caused me to raise my eyebrows. I looked over at Deion's intense expression with a puzzled look on my face. I knew he wasn't going to agree to what Hector was proposing.

Looking over at my face, Hector said, "Bella, do you have any input on this?"

"I don't mean any disrespect, but we are taking all the risks, and I understand the situation with Rico has you second-guessing, but we did recover," I said, continuing to express my thoughts.

"Smart and beautiful. I like that." He smiled. "What do you propose?"

I broke down what would be profitable for both sides, including the cost to fix Rico's situation. I reached in my purse, pulling out a pen, and wrote a figure on my napkin before showing it to Deion, who slid it to Hector.

Looking at the napkin, Hector placed his hand on his chin, nodding in agreement. "That's fair and very wise, Miss Bella. You have a good sense of business."

"So, are we in business?" Deion asked.

"Give me a few days to think about it. Kat will contact you."

The waitress walked over with our food, passing each of us our plate. We started eating while engaging in a light conversation for the remainder of the dinner. After about two hours, it was time to go. Hector reached out to shake Deion's hand, then spoke to me.

"Bella, it was a pleasure."

"The pleasure was all mine, Mr. Ramirez."

"Hector," he corrected.

"Hector," I said, nodding. I could tell that Deion was furious.

Once we were out of the restaurant, Deion let loose. "What was all that shit, Bella?"

"What?" I rolled my eyes. "The deal needed to be closed, and clearly you was about to agree to some fuck shit . . . so I stepped in."

"I had the shit covered, Bella. You were supposed to fall back," he said, handing the attendant the ticket for the car.

"No, I was supposed to be on a getaway with my man. You were on some fuck shit, though," I shot back. "Nigga, let's not forget you had me in this club," I continued. "You thought I didn't peep that shit." The valet pulled up with the car. I hopped into the passenger seat and folded my arms across my chest.

The following morning, I got up, still mad. "Deion, wake up.Wake up, nigga."

"What, Bella? Damn."

"I thought we were a team."

"It's too early for this shit."

"Fuck that," I said, pulling the covers off the bed. "You're making moves out here by yourself, then expecting me to agree to the bullshit. I'm tired of saving your dumb ass."

"Oooh, have you forgotten how you even learned this shit?"

"Yeah, ight, Deion. I'm going the fuck home. You can stay out here by your motherfucking self."

"Ain't nobody stopping you, bitch," Deion said furiously

"You are absolutely right," I said, packing my shit. "Fuck you and that ho," I said, walking out of the hotel room.

Chapter 14

Arriving home, I felt utterly drained. Before tending to the baby, I needed a few moments to rest my eyes. Turning on my phone, I discovered no missed messages from Deion. This time, I had to be the one to leave. Deion's absurd attitude necessitated action. Without hesitation, I dialed my aunt Pam.

"Hi, Auntie, how are you doing?"

"I'm okay, Bella. How are you?"

"Well, I'm calling to see if me and Junior can come to stay with you a few days."

"That shouldn't be a problem. Is everything okay?"

"Yes. We should be there this evening."

"Okay, baby, I will see y'all later," she said before hanging up.

It was time that Deion felt my pressure at this moment. I didn't have much to lose, and hopefully, Deion would miss us enough to change. Packing a few clothes to last for a week, I got ready to head over to Nikki's to pick up Junior.

Time was not on my side. I needed to pick up the baby and be on my way, not wanting to get stuck at Nikki's. I knocked on the door, and Nikki answered with a surprised look on her face.

"Wuzzup, bitch? Y'all back early?"

"Naw, I'm back early. I came to pick up the baby," I said, walking in the house.

"What happened?" she said as she headed to the back to grab Junior.

"Nothing. I'm just a tired, girl," I replied, gathering up his things. I grabbed his baby bag off the table and placed the items inside.

"Well, it will all work out. You and Deion will bounce back," Nikki said as she walked back into the living room. "Uh, damn, bitch. You got him back and ready to go."

"Girl, I wanna lay down," I said, reaching for the baby. "Maybe that was the problem. I kept letting shit slide, without requiring change long-term. Anyway, girl, thank you. I'm about to head home," I said, grabbing his bag and heading to the car.

I opened the back passenger door, strapped the baby in, then threw his bag on the floor of the car. I waved to Nikki as she watched me get in the car and pull off.

It took about three hours to get to my aunt's house in Amherst. Pulling up, I was amazed by how gorgeous the area was. The grass was green, with lilies all across the front of the house. I got out of the car, grabbed the baby, and walked to the door. Taking a deep breath, inhaling the fresh air, I rang the doorbell. It only took a few moments before she opened the door.

Pam was my favorite out of all my mom's sisters. She had long, dark hair with deep waves and a china doll face. Slim but still thick, with big boobs and incredible hips, she still looked fantastic at her age.

"Hey, baby, do you need any help?" she asked, grabbing Junior and walking into the house.

"No, I got it."

"Hey, Auntie's baby. You are getting big." She smiled as she took off his jacket.

I went to the car, got our bags, and headed back into the house. The smell of lasagna hit my nose, making my mouth water as I placed my bags near the stairs.

"Auntie, it smells good in here."

"You must be hungry. Go wash up, and I'll fix you and the baby's plates."

"Okay," I said as I headed to the bathroom.

When I got into the kitchen, my aunt was already feeding Junior. She had placed my plate on the counter.

"What's going on, Bella?"

"Whatcha mean?"

"When do you call me to ask to stay for a couple of days?"

"Can we please talk about it later? I have to run outside for a moment."

Three days later, I walked outside to grab something out of the car, when I saw a piece of paper on the windshield. Shutting the door, I pulled the letter out and read each word out loud. "Bella, I hope this letter finds you in good health and prosperity. Meet me down the block."

"This nigga crazy. He can't be here," I mumbled, folding the paper up and placing it in my pocket. A thousand and one things were running through my mind.

Taking in the sights, I hopped in the car and pulled off. *How did he know where I was?* I thought as I approached the truck at the end of the block. Pulling up behind it, I parked and got out of the car with a fuck-you attitude as I nonchalantly approached the SUV. I froze mid-step as Hector stepped out.

"Bella, stunning as ever."

"How did you—" I started, looking around.

"I had you followed since our dinner. I saw the tension between you and Deion," he said with a slight smirk.

"Hector, now, why would you do that? I am quite capable of handling Deion."

"My point exactly. I'm offering you a spot at the table. You will be a major part of the East Coast organization, and I have to ensure my assets."

"I'm confused. What?"

"You're going to run the East Coast, and I'm going to train you."

"What about Deion and Kat?"

"He is good, but clearly you're a better fit. Come get in the truck. I have something to show you."

Hesitant, I turned my head around nervously, looking in the direction of my auntie's house. Hector reached out for my hand, then calmly escorted me to the truck. I sat in silence for a moment as he pulled off. He turned the corner and then broke the silence.

"Bella, I need you to trust me," he said as we turned another corner.

"Trust you, huh?"

"Yes. Here is just a piece of what is to come," he said as he pulled out a set of keys from his suit jacket. "This is yours if you want it. Sometimes it is good for the left hand not to know what the right hand's got in play," he stated. "I will not tell Deion nor Kat about this location."

Opening the palm of my hand, I accepted the keys, still unsure if I should trust him. "Do you know what you're asking of me?"

"Yes. You will do just fine, Bella. When I'm done, you will be colder than winter," he said with confidence. "But remember, you have to remain the same with Deion until further notice." He pulled up to a gorgeous new construction at 88 Hubbarston Place. I was speechless as a sense of security came over me.

"The house will be finished in three weeks. I will furnish it and let you know when it's ready," he said, pulling off as we turned the corner back to my truck.

Sliding out of Hector's truck, I was still on cloud nine. Jumping back into my own truck, I pulled off, heading back to my aunt's place. When I walked in, the aroma of roast from the crockpot hit me like a ton of bricks. Heading into the living room, I found her and Junior sound asleep on the couch. I walked into my room with a heavy mind and heart, pulling the keys Hector gave me out of my pocket.

The next few days brought a refreshing break—no incessant phone ringing, no knocks at the door, no police encounters, and no pressure. It was a much-needed getaway, offering a chance to clear my head. What the hell was Deion up to? I still hadn't heard from him, and truthfully, I didn't make an effort to call him either.

A week passed, and he finally texted me early Sunday morning.

Deion: Where are you?

Bella: Oh, it took you a week to text me?

Deion: Bitch, stop playing with me. You and my son better bring y'all asses back here before dark. We don't have time for this shit. Hector is ready to do business.

Bella: Fuck you, Deion.

Deion: Bella, I'm sorry. What the fuck! We in this together. Just come home.

Bella: So now we a team?

The delay in his response had me second-guessing his motives. My blood was boiling as I paced back and forth.

"Baby, is everything okay?" my aunt asked, seeing the stress on my face.

"No, Auntie. Deion has me frustrated."

"What happened?" she asked.

"Nothing," I replied, still pacing.

She walked out of the living room and returned, sitting on the couch and patting the seat next to her for me to sit down. Smacking my lips, I complied. She opened her hand, and a little blue pill sat in the center of her palm.

"Here, Bella. Try this," she told me. "It will make you feel better."

I opened my hand, and she dropped the little blue pill in my palm. Not even ten minutes after swallowing it, I felt no animosity or anger anymore.

Then, I became drowsy, so I rested my head on the arm of the couch and closed my eyes. All feelings had disappeared out of my body. I have never felt so warm and fuzzy, as if I was walking on cloud nine, dreaming of 88 Hubbardston Place.

I woke up the following day, stretched out on the couch with a comforter over me. Knowing Deion would be upset, I called. When he answered, I could tell from his dry tone that he had an issue with us not being home.

"Hey," he said dryly.

"Morning. We coming home, okay?"

"About time. I'll see y'all shortly. I love you."

"Me too," I said, hanging up. I started packing everything, and when I was done, I walked in the kitchen to find my aunt sitting at the table.

"Hey, Auntie," I said, sitting down next to her.

"Hey, babe, you are all packed and ready to go."

"Yes, ma'am, but I need one more favor," I said, sliding her the key that Hector gave me. "This key is to the house at eighty-eight Hubbardston Place. In three weeks, I need you to rent it out to a nice ole lady. Now, I will need you to manage it, and anything you need, take it out of the rent and save the rest for me."

"Bella, where did you get—" she started to inquire but stopped herself. "I won't ask you any questions today, but just know I will want you to tell me what is going on next time I see you. But I will do as you ask and won't tell a soul," she said, securing the key in her hand.

"Thank you, and yes, ma'am, I will," I assured her before getting up and grabbing the bags. I put everything in the car and came back in for Junior. "I love you, Auntie, and thanks again," I said, reaching for the baby before leaving out the door.

The drive back to the crib had me thinking, *I have to play my cards right.* I couldn't let Hector down.

Chapter 15

About two months had passed, and my birthday was nearing. Nikki and I still managed to go shopping, but I had to make sure shit was on point with this new arrangement with Hector, Deion, and Kat.

Later that night, we decided to hit the Jamaican club to celebrate early. While we were at the bar, Sammy decided to meet us there to drink with his little sister. It was nice to see my brother step out and celebrate with me. After about an hour, Sammy told me he was about to take off.

"Yo, Sammy, can we come with you?" I asked.

"I don't care."

"Let me drop my car off. I don't need Deion tripping."

"Let's roll."

We walked into a house party, bobbing our heads as music was blasting from everywhere. Nikki and I spotted a black round table in the center to have a seat when a white dude walked over, dumping cocaine on it.

"What the fuck?" I said as we looked at each other.

Quickly, Sammy came over to the table, telling the guy that we were not allowed to get down with them. He moved us to another table in the corner. We scanned the room as we smoked our bud and laughed for the next few hours.

As I sat back and took in all the festivities, my money wheels started churning. *We could move that shit Hector is giving us in no time in this bitch,* I thought, watching the party progress around me.

Just then, Sammy walked over to our table, high as hell.

"Okay, shit 'bout to get real in the bitch. Y'all cab is outside."

We looked at him with our hands on our hips. "Seriously, Sammy?"

"Yeah, Bella, go 'head now," he said, handing me money.

"Whatever," I said, reaching for the money and leaving.

The following day, my stomach was sour. I saw Deion was already out of bed. *Shit!* I sat up quickly, forgetting Nikki had stayed the night. Jumping out of bed, I went to the living room. Nikki looked up and rolled her eyes at me. At that point, I knew Deion was acting funny just off Nikki's vibe. He came from the kitchen with Junior in his arms, and the motion in his walk told me that he was on some shit.

"Good morning, y'all," I said before the urge to throw up invaded my body. Quickly walking past Deion, I headed to the bathroom, just barely making it to the toilet. Trying to pull it together, I washed my face and brushed my teeth before walking back into the living room. I heard Nikki telling Deion about last night. I was glad she knew how to break the ice because I knew Deion was upset with me.

"What time did you get in?" Deion asked her.

"Maybe three or somewhere around there."

Deion shook his head as he handed me our son. I could see he was still in his feelings as I placed Junior in his playpen. *I guess I have to give this nigga some pussy. Maybe that will change his attitude,* I thought.

"Nikki, that shit was crazy last night," I said, walking back into the kitchen.

"Yes, girl. I have never seen that before, so many people snorting coke."

"Naw, Sammy is a nut, girl. Acting like we not grown."

Looking in the fridge, I grabbed some shrimp and made some grits to go with it. While I was cooking, I told Nikki to roll up as we continued talking about last night.

"Shiid, bitch, imagine how much money that would be if I started selling to their asses. Just think about it."

"Bittccchhh, Deion is not about to let you do that, so don't even think about it."

"We'll see," I said while fixing our plates.

After we ate, I dropped Nikki off at home and went right back to my house. I knew I couldn't make any pit stops. When I walked in, Deion had made himself a plate and was at the table eating. I sat at the table and decided to bring up my idea about selling to Sammy's friends at their parties.

"That party was live, and it got me thinking. We should look into selling coke as well. We don't always gotta cook for niggas, Deion. Let them cook they own shid."

He looked at me sideways as if I had two heads. "Bella, why are you trying to change shit now? The way I have things set up is working just fine."

Looking away, I started watching television. I could see that he wasn't feeling my idea, making it clear again. I just let it go.

My phone started ringing. Looking down, I saw it was my mom. Our relationship had started getting better. We didn't talk all the time, but she would call me once a week, or I would call her.

Picking up the phone, I said, "Hey, mom."

"Hello, baby. Are you busy?"

"No, what's up?"

"Can you ride with me real quick?"

"Yeah. Let me get Junior ready, okay?"

"Okay," she said before hanging up.

Not even fifteen minutes later, my mom pulled up. Once we pulled off, my mom started to talk. She was a little jittery, so I was curious about what was going on.

"I'm moving to California," she blurted out.

I looked at her as if she was crazy. She was talking so fast at this point that I had to tell her to slow down and repeat herself. I didn't think I heard what she was saying, or maybe I didn't want to hear her.

"Jake is out of control," she said, glancing at me with those crystal blue eyes. "Since he got off parole last June, he has been getting high. I know he smokes bud and maybe throws a few beers back, but this new shit he's doing is a problem."

"Why are y'all moving to Cali?"

"We need to, Bella," she said with a high pitch in her voice as her eyes got watery.

"Okay," was my only response. When I saw that, I knew she was dead-ass serious. I said nothing else.

"Jake has been snorting and shooting up coke. Yes, I have dabbled with him here and there, but now we just need a fresh start."

I shook my head as rage came over my body. "What?" I spat, confused. She had been an alcoholic for years, washing her misery down her throat. It took her a long time to get on the right track, and to hear she was now doing drugs was a big issue. I listened closely, with disappointment all over my face, as she explained their situation.

"Just take us home," I said, annoyed as I looked down at my phone, noticing a text had just come in.

Hector: Miss Bella, how are you?

Scratching my head, I replied. Bella: Everything okay?

Hector: Yes. How are the candy bars moving?

Bella: Great. Everyone loves "Chocolate."

Hector: I will be coming into town next week. Can we meet?

Bella: That shouldn't be a problem.

Not paying attention, I saw we were in front of my house. As I was getting Junior out of the car, my mom knew I was disappointed, but I didn't want to make her feel any less.

"I love you, Ma. I'll call you later, okay?"

"I love you too, baby." She sniffled as she blew her nose.

When I got in the house, I saw Deion was watching television. He immediately got up and helped me with Junior. He saw the hurt on my face as I handed the baby to him.

"It was rough with Momma," I told him.

"You know I'm here," Deion said.

I smirked at him and headed to the room. I just couldn't believe what my mom was doing. How could she? Why would she leave her family?

I needed to clear my head and figure out a way to get Deion on board. I turned on the radio to 93.7 WBLK to rock out while I smoked a joint. About an hour later, I walked back into the living room. Deion and Junior were asleep on the couch.

I picked up my son, placing him close to my chest as he let out a low cry. Patting his back slowly, I walk into the kitchen to make him a bottle before putting him to bed. Easing my way to Junior's room, I placed him in his crib, covering him as he started to whimper.

Patting his Pamper, I watched as he quickly went back to sleep. I left the door slightly open so that I could hear him. Walking back into the living room, I stood in front of Deion, admiring him as he slept on the couch.

Hmmm, no sleep for you, daddy.

Lowering myself to my knees, I put my hair up in a messy bun, smiling. Pulling out his semi-hard dick, I spit in my palms for lubricant as I wrapped my hands around all of his thick meat. Pacing my motion, I got it nice and wet. I picked up speed, swallowing him inch by inch until my tongue touched his base.

"Bella. Bella, don't. Stop," he moaned as he put his hands on my head.

Gaining more momentum and coming back up, I started jacking off his dick while keeping the same speed, bobbing my head up and down as his juices ran down my face.

"I fuckin' love you," he said.

As I was about to finish him off, I could feel the intensity of his veins as they started to bulge. Deion quickly lifted my chin. Leaning in, he kissed me on my lips as he proceeded to stand. Picking my little ass up, he placed me on the back of the couch. I spread my legs, holding my ankles. Deion spit on my pussy as he devours my twat like it was his last meal.

"Stick your finger in my ass," I whispered. "Ugh . . . aww . . . yes daddy, just like that," I said as Deion eased his finger in my ass while still sucking my clit.

"Oh, God!" I yelled. My legs couldn't stop shaking, and my eyes were rolling as my heart was racing.

Switching positions, Deion flipped me over the arm of the couch with my ass in the air, arching my back. He slid deeper up in me.

"Ugh . . . yes . . . yes . . . Deion, fuck me."

Grabbing my hair with force and pulling my head back, he pounded this pussy. We both came at the same time. My body was hot and tingly all over. I couldn't move. I was so exhausted. Rolling over, I lit up a Newport.

Deion walked to the bathroom to wash up. He came back out and washed me as well.

This is why I fucks with him. He can be so sweet when he wants to.

As he passed my drink to me, I turned on the television to watch a movie as he started rolling up a blunt. Deion gave me the blunt, and I hit it a few times before my eyes got heavy, and I drifted off.

The next day, I was still in my feelings. I feel weak when I'm not in control. I folded my arms across my chest. I tried letting it slide, but the more I looked at Deion, I felt my face turn beet red as my nose flared up.

"I have something I need to tell you," I said in a stern voice.

"Spit it out, Bella."

"I think I'm pregnant."

"What? What did you say?" he asked.

"I think I'm pregnant, Deion."

Wrapping his arms around me, he embraced me tightly. He was super excited, kissing me on my forehead while rubbing my belly.

I tried to explain that I didn't think it was a good idea to have this baby and that we should think it through, but this nigga went in on me.

"This my motherfucking baby. We're keeping this baby," he yelled. "What type of shit you on, Bella?"

"I'm trying to reason with you. I thought it was hard with one baby under two years old, so I know it would get harder with another one."

Deion was mad as fuck. His whole body shifted as he leaned in my face, jabbing his finger in my dimple before yelling, "We are having this baby." He walked out and slammed the door behind him.

I broke down after he left, feeling like my life would be over if I had this baby.

Chapter 16

The cold, sterile walls of the exam room seemed to close in on me as Dr. Barnes prepared to check on our baby. My mind raced with conflicting emotions—aggravation, fear, and a hint of reluctant excitement. Deion's joy, however, was blinding, his enthusiasm contagious.

"Ugh, this the shit I don't want to be doing, Deion," I grumbled, frustration vibrating in my voice.

Deion's eyes widened, his excitement undeterred. "What's that?"

"Never mind. Can you go get me some water, please?" I sighed, hoping the brief distraction would ease my nerves.

Deion quickly left the room and returned with a Dixie cup of water, handing it to me as the doctor walked in with a smile that seemed to match Deion's enthusiasm. I rolled my eyes, sipping the water and forcing a smile as I handed back the balled-up cup.

"I hear we're having a baby. Let's take a look and a little listen, Bella," Dr. Barnes said, donning a pair of latex gloves.

I nodded, the weight of the moment sinking in. Dr. Barnes examined me, and then, with a swift motion, she pulled a small black rectangular box with a speaker attached out of her pocket. Placing the speaker on my belly, she turned up the volume, and soon, the room was filled with the rhythmic sound of our baby's heartbeat.

"Is that my baby?" Deion's eyes widened, a genuine smile lighting up his face. "That's a strong heartbeat there," he marveled, his tough exterior momentarily melting away. As the room resonated with the steady thumping, a sense of connection overcame us. Deion's joy mirrored the rapid beats echoing through the small device, and for the first time in a long while, I allowed myself to feel a flicker of hope. The heartbeat, a tangible sign of life, bridged the gap between our past and the uncertain future, uniting us in the journey ahead.

As Dr. Barnes detailed the prenatal plan, I struggled to absorb the information. *Twelve weeks along.* The weight of those words sank in as I got dressed, my mind racing with a mix of emotions. I felt floored, unable to comprehend the reality of my situation. A second child, a different path, and an uncertain future stretched before me.

I can only hope to have a girl at this point, I thought, clinging to the glimmer of optimism that maybe, just maybe, a daughter could bring a sense of completeness to my fractured world.

The memory of Deja, the daughter I had lost, lingered in the corners of my mind. We never talked about her, as if acknowledging her existence would open a floodgate of pain. Now, with the decision to keep the baby, it felt like my life was once again put on hold, and I couldn't shake the feeling of being trapped.

Months passed, and we moved to a new apartment, attempting to start fresh. However, the new space never felt like home. Deion's cousin, a familiar face from Rochester, became a temporary addition, helping us navigate the complexities of the life we had chosen. Deion, consumed by the day-to-day operations, gradually kept me at arm's length, leaving me to manage the numbers on my own.

Frustration built up within me, compounded by the weight of my seven-month pregnancy. I was tired, both physically and emotionally, yet Deion's focus on the money left me feeling neglected and alone. Hormones raged through my body, intensifying the already turbulent emotions. As I navigated the challenges of my pregnancy, the strain on our relationship became more evident. The quest for stability, the shadow of our past, and the complexity of our present collided, leaving me grappling with a sense of isolation and realization that the path ahead was uncertain and fraught with challenges.

I grabbed my phone off the nightstand and texted my aunt Pam to check on the house and tenant.

Bella: Hey, Auntie, everything ok?

Pam: Hey, sweetie! Yes, and I have a nice little something off to the side. How is Auntie's new little bundle doing?

Bella: The baby is doing well, Auntie. I will try to get up and see you soon.

Pam: Okay, sweetness. I will be here. Just let me know.

Shortly after I checked in with my aunt, I wondered if Nikki wanted to come by and hang out.

Bitch, come through. I texted, waiting for her response.

Nikki: On my way.

Bella: I will be outside waiting, lol I texted before placing my phone on the nightstand. I jumped up and got dressed with excitement.

The air outside was thick with the familiar scent of the neighborhood as Nikki pulled up in her car. I was already dressed and ready to go, my decision to leave without telling Deion echoing in the uneasy silence between us. When Nikki arrived, we exchanged a quick nod, and without uttering a word, I slid into the passenger seat. The engine roared to life as we pulled away from the house, leaving behind the tension that lingered within those walls.

As we drove, Nikki and I decided to make a pit stop, copping some weed to set the tone for the day. The familiar rituals of the hood embraced us as we navigated through the streets, heading toward Sammy's place in the Sweet Wood projects. When we arrived, I stepped out of the car and looked around, taking in the sights of the neighborhood.

"Damn, this nigga loves the hood," I mumbled, a mix of nostalgia and weariness in my voice. The familiar faces and the gritty atmosphere were a stark reminder of a life I had both embraced and tried to escape.

Sammy's place held a unique energy, a blend of camaraderie and street wisdom. As we entered, the air buzzed with conversations and the low hum of music. I found a spot, settling in as Nikki and I immersed ourselves in the atmosphere of Sweet Wood.

The decision to leave without a word to Deion still weighed on me, but in that moment, surrounded by the familiar sights and sounds of the hood, I allowed myself a brief respite from the complexities of my life. We walked in the house, high as hell. Sammy was in the kitchen, cooking.

"Wuzzup? The fuck, nigga, you cooking now and shit?"

"Hell yeah. What the fuck y'all into?"

"Shid," Nikki said.

"Aye, Nikki, you remember when this nigga left us stranded at the bar?" I said, smacking my lips.

"Hell yeah," she said as she busted out laughing.

Sammy laughed, throwing the kitchen towel toward me. "Why you always bring up some ole shit, Bella?"

"Why you always get us into some bullshit? Man, we were chilling at the bar." Cracking a smile, we all busted out laughing.

Next thing I knew, Alicia burst through the door, screaming, "Give me my fucking keys."

Clearing my throat, I said, "On a serious note, Sammy, I need your help."

"Whatcha need from me, sis?"

"I want to know more about the parties. I might have an idea."

"What do you have in mind?"

"I saw everyone snorting coke. Who is supplying it? And how good is it?"

"A cat from out of town be over dere. It's good, too. Why?"

"Bella, are you going there with Sammy?" Nikki interrupted.

"Why not, Nikki?"

"Deion. That's why not."

"Girl, I'm only asking, damn."

"Yeah, a'ight."

Nikki knew how to kill my mood. Looking at the clock on the wall, I saw it was getting late, and I needed to get back to the house. "Aye, Sammy, I'm 'bout to get up out of here. I have to get the baby," I said.

"Ight, sis. Nikki, y'all be safe."

We said our goodbyes and left.

Getting into the car, I asked, "Nikki, why do you always gotta bring up Deion?"

"Clearly you don't think things through, Bella," she replied.

"You really don't have a clue how I am thinking sometimes. I feel like you team Deion," I told her.

"I know you fucking lying. Bella, I've gone against the grain for you. My family still acts funny toward me," she said angrily. "And you really know you don't trust Sammy like that. Why would you even consider putting him on?"

Sucking my teeth, I said, "Yeah, you feel how you feel, and I'ma stand on what I said about Deion. As far as Sammy, it's not about putting him on. It's about him putting me on with his circle. But you know everything, Nikki."

She turned the music up and pulled off. I could tell she was pissed, and I didnt care.

We were almost at the house and my phone rang.

"Hey, Deion."

"We just leave without saying anything?" he asked.

"Nigga, I'm about to pull up. Don't start, because you don't always tell me when you leave," I said.

"Ight, I see you when you get here," he replied, hanging up.

I looked back up. We were in the driveway. I ain't say nothing to Nikki as I got out. I just shut the door and walked in the house. The smell of pizza and wings filled my nose. *Good, I don't have to cook,* I thought.

"Hey, where is the baby?" I asked Deion.

"He fell asleep while eating his pizza. I laid him down," he said.

"Oh, okay, good," I said, kicking my shoes off and getting on the couch. I was exhausted.

"Do you want some pizza or wings, bae?" Deion asked.

"Naw, I'ma head up to bed in a minute. Are you coming?"

The sound of shattering glass jolted me out of my sleep. I grabbed my phone off the nightstand to see what time it was. Looking over at Deion, who was still sound asleep, I got up and went to the bathroom. Once I was finished, I quickly washed my hands and started to open the door when I heard the stairs creak.

I paused for a moment to listen. Then I crept toward the window and peeked outside. When I didn't see anything, I slowly opened the door to go back to bed. As I exited the bathroom, I was met with a cold piece of steel against my forehead. I froze, trying to stay calm as I let out a whimper. Before my eyes could blink a second time, the intruder took the gun and slapped me across my face, causing me to fall back into the bathroom wall. I screamed as the blood started dripping down my cheek.

"Bitch, shut the fuck up before I shut you up! Where the fuck is the money and work?" he barked, pointing the pistol in my direction.

"Fuck you, nigga," I spat, grabbing the side of my face.

The masked intruder stepped forward, hovering over me as he pulled my hair and dragged me back down the hallway. I could feel the carpet burning my backside as he pulled me into the room before dropping me near the bottom of the bed. I sat up, cradling my belly.

He leaned over and whispered, "I told you I would never let you go."

Instantly, my heart dropped to my stomach when I heard Tyrell's voice. I looked over and saw Deion tied up in his boxers on the floor near the dresser. Tears rolled down my eyes. Instantly, I regretted that night I slept with Tyrell last year. I was so confused about what was going on as a feeling of betrayal surged through my body. I couldn't believe he would do this to me.

"Tell me where the muthafuckin' money is and the work," he yelled again, swinging his pistol back and forth between the both of us.

Deion's face turned cold. "What money you talkin' about, nigga?" he said, spitting out the blood that accumulated in his mouth.

With the pistol pointed at my belly, his tone changed to a deadly echo that pulsated through my body.

"No, not my baby! Deion, tell them where the shit is. Just give it to them," I pleaded, not understanding why he was so hesitant. Deion took one last look at my bloody face before Tyrell's partner raised his gun.

Pop! Pop!

All I saw was a flash. Everything around me was surreal and moving in slow motion. I screamed Deion's name from the top of my lungs.

Tyrell and his partner took off running downstairs. I crawled to find my phone, then to Deion as I broke down crying, trying to dial 911. I held on tight to Deion as he struggled to tell me he loved me.

"Help is on the way. Stay with me," I said, covering his body with mine.

"I can hear the sirens, baby. Please hold on. Fuck!" I cried. Deion was losing so much blood, and his breathing had weakened. "Shit, they're taking forever," I yelled. It felt like the time was slipping away as I applied pressure to his chest. I was so scared.

The chaotic whirlwind of events unfolded rapidly, each moment laden with fear, uncertainty, and a desperate plea to a higher power. The wailing sirens signaled the arrival of the EMTs, and I rushed to convey the urgency of the situation.

"We're upstairs. Hurry, he's dying!" I shouted, my heart pounding in my chest as the paramedics stormed into the room. Desperation clung to my words as I fervently asked God not to take him away.

The paramedics swiftly took charge, moving Deion onto a gurney and rushing him out the door. Their barrage of questions overwhelmed me, leaving my mind in a chaotic fog. In the midst of the chaos, I managed to call my mom, updating her on the unfolding crisis. She assured me she'd take care of Junior until things settled.

Arriving at the hospital, I became aware of the concerned gazes and inquiries about my well-being. The realization hit me. Tyrell's violent attack had left visible wounds on me, and I likely needed medical attention. A nurse guided me to a wheelchair, leading me to a room where another nurse assessed the damages on my face. In the midst of pain, whether from my head injury or the contractions, I couldn't distinguish one ache from another. The nurse, glancing at the baby monitor, informed me that I was in labor.

"I can't be," I protested, desperation in my voice. "I need to go check on my man!"

"I'm sorry, ma'am," the nurse empathized, preparing to take me to the third floor. "You're not alone. I'm right here with you."

The contractions intensified, and the reality sank in—I couldn't do this alone. Frustration, fear, and pain mingled as the nurse reassured me. "Deion needs to be here. Fuccckkk!" I screamed, the waves of contractions relentless.

Four hours later, in the midst of agony and chaos, Jhai Lee Jackson was born, a testament to resilience amid the storm. At 19 inches long, weighing 9 pounds and 8 ounces, he entered the world. Another king had arrived.

"Congratulations. I told you that you could do it," the nurse said, offering a glimmer of comfort.

As they took my baby for examination, the exhaustion, excitement, and drugs combined pulled me into a dreamless sleep. The hospital room, once a battleground of emotions, now echoed with the slight hum of monitors and the quiet breaths of a newborn, a fragile piece of serenity in the aftermath of the storm.

Chapter 17

The air in Deion's room felt heavy with tension, and his distant demeanor set off alarm bells in my mind. As I leaned down to kiss his cheek, the awkwardness in his stare caught me off guard.

"Hey, baby. Are you okay? How you feelin' today?" I inquired, hoping for a reassuring response.

"'Sup, Bella," he replied, his gaze avoiding mine. "I'm good. How are the kids?"

"They're good. Over at Nikki's," I responded, feeling a pang of unease at his lack of warmth. "The doctor said you'd be home in a week." I sat on the edge of his bed, sensing an undercurrent of something unsettling.

"Bella, did you find out anything new about what went down?" Deion asked, his tone carrying an edge of urgency.

"I told you, some guys broke into the house and tried to rob us. They pistol-whipped me and shot you because you wouldn't give them the work and money," I explained, my frustration growing. Standing up, I stared out the window, unable to contain the burning question inside me.

"Deion, why didn't you just give everything up? They had a gun to my belly. This is not making any sense."

"Shit, I couldn't. I've been pushing weight for this guy," he admitted, and my confusion deepened.

"I know. I'm not talking about Hector."

"I'm not talking about Hector either."

"Deion, what the fuck is going on? What are you not telling me?" I demanded, folding my arms. His demeanor shifted abruptly, throwing me off even more. His next words hit me like a gut punch.

"No, Bella," he said in a low voice. "You don't understand. I've been pushing weight for this nigga named Perez, but, Bella, he ain't just any nigga. He's an undercover police officer, and now I think he is trying to set me up."

"What did you say?" I asked in disbelief. "Fuck, fuck! Nah," I muttered, shaking my head. "There is no way you are working with the boys knowing we're working with Hector. How? When? What were you thinking? Our family could be in danger," I yelled.

"Shut the fuck up and listen. Damn, Bella," Deion snapped, raising his voice.

"I can't believe you would do this to us," I said, turning around and walking out. The weight of unanswered questions and the betrayal from both Tyrell and Deion left me struggling to hold back tears. At that moment, I was heading home with the heaviest heart I had ever had.

Pulling into the driveway, I let out a heavy sigh, leaning my head back on the headrest as the tears continued to fall. *Get yo' shit together, bitch,* I thought as I pulled Dion's gun out of the glove compartment and exited the car.

Before opening the front door, I glanced out the window, and two cards fell to the ground: Niagara County Department of Social Services and Niagara County Police Department. The stark reality of consequences confronted me.

"What's next?" I screamed, walking in the house and closing the door. Sitting on the couch, I placed the gun next to me and immediately broke down.

***

The next couple of days were crazy. I immediately got a hold of Child Protective Services before going to see Deion. They wanted to set up an appointment to come and check on the kids, and I agreed. When I walked into his cold and gloomy room, Deion was in the chair, having lunch.

"How are you feeling?" I smiled.

"I could be doing better," Deion replied. "Why didn't you bring the boys to see me?"

"Why would I do that? I already have CPS on my ass from your shooting. I don't think Junior needs to see you like this anyway."

"Fuck you mean, Bella? You don't think that I need to see them?"

"It ain't about you. It's about them."

"I'm so sorry, Bella," he said, lowering his tone.

"What are you sorry for exactly?" I asked, smacking my lips. "Are you sorry for not telling me what was going on with the business, or for putting me and the kids' lives in danger? Or how about Kat?" I asked, fighting back the tears.

"I'ma keep it deadass real witcha, Bella."

"Go head, nigga. I'm listening," I told him, crossing my arms.

Swiping the top of his head, Deion took in a deep breath. Pushing the tray table to the side, he cuffed his hands in front of him and explained. "I just had a feeling we were being watched. I was for sure it was just a gut feeling."

I just looked at him as he kept going.

"One night, a car got behind me and started following me. I just did a pickup from the spot on south."

"So, you knew someone was watching?"

"I mean, I had a feeling, I didn't know for sure. Let me finish. It was like they already knew I was holding, I thought it was some stick-up boys or some shit. I bent a corner or two trying to shake 'em. As soon as I got a block away, I saw lights behind me, so I pulled over."

Smacking my lips, I said, "What happened next?"

"This white nigga gets out walks up to my window and tells me, 'Pop the trunk, Deion.' I swear on God, Bella, he knew my name."

"You sound real crazy right now." All I could do was stare at Deion with a puzzled look.

Oh, this nigga think I'm stupid, I thought, shaking my head.

"Why you, ain't say nothing when it went down? Where were you coming from again, and when was this?" I asked.

"I know how you are," Deion said.

"I feel like I'm missing something from this story, Deion. What happened with the white nigga?"

"He gave me two choices, go to jail or work for him. You see I'm not in jail. What's crazy is, Kat had me come by before I stopped on south. She had a new drop-off location."

"Word," I said, looking at him. At this moment, my woman's intuition kicked in. He was fucking Kat.

"Why are you making this a big deal?" Deion asked.

"Make it make sense, Deion. Out of the blue, you're working with the cops, and you're meeting Kat alone," I said, pissed off.

"You're getting off the subject," he scolded. "Perez's prices are lower, and I know what I'm dealing with."

"Oh, so now you're making moves without me?"

"It's not like that, Bella. I saw an opportunity, and I took it."

"Fuck you, Deion," I said. "You know you're wrong in this situation, and if the roles were reversed, you would feel some type of way too."

"Bella, don't be like this. I need you more than anything right now."

"Like I said, Deion, fuck you. Nigga, you got me messed up for real," I spat while walking out.

If he thinks I am down, he has another thing coming, and I know for sure he fucking Kat now, I thought as I was heading home.

Pulling into my driveway, I noticed a gray Impala pulling up. "Who is this?" I mumbled as the car turned into my driveway. Looking in my rearview mirror, I watched as the man opened his door and stepped out.

Getting out of my car, I hit my alarm. "Can I help you?"

"Excuse me, Miss Goins. Do you have time to answer a few questions?"

"Who are you?" I asked, turning my nose up as the stale smell of Old Spice attacked me.

"My name is Officer Raymose Perez. May we go inside to talk about the shooting a few weeks ago?"

I was hesitant at first, but then I obliged. As Perez followed me into the house, my stomach started feeling uneasy.

"What do you remember from that night?" he asked, sitting on the couch.

"Not much. It was kinda hazy. Maybe two or three men were in my house. One pistol-whipped me, and then shots went off."

"Did you happen to see their faces? Did they take anything?"

"No . . . I don't think so. Why?"

Standing up, Perez handed me his card. "If you remember anything, give me a call."

"Yeah, a'ight," I said, pretending I had no idea who he was. *What the hell does he want?*

Hearing him mumble something as he walked out of the house, I said, "Excuse me?"

He turned around. His eyes were ice-cold as he gave me the grimmest smile. "You enjoy the rest of your day, ma'am."

Slamming the door and locking it behind him, I stood there for a second. My phone started ringing. It was Hector.

"Miss Goins, can we meet?"

"Hello, Hector. What's going on?"

"I need to talk to you in person."

"I can't right now. Something has come up."

"Is everything okay?"

"Yes. I'm sorry, Hector. There's somebody at the door. Can we finish this later?"

"I'm only here these next three days. Meet me at the house tomorrow night."

"Okay," I said, hanging up the phone.

"Who is it?" I yelled, walking toward the door.

"It's me, Nikki. Girl, open this door."

"I'm sorry," I said, unlocking the door before pulling it open.

"What's good, bitch?" she said, walking in and placing the baby's car seat on the floor, along with his diaper bag and Junior's backpack.

"Girl, I can't call it. It's been a long day. You want a glass of wine?"

"Sure do, and I'll roll up."

After getting my kids situated, I walked into the kitchen and grabbed the wine out of the fridge. My mind was racing as I gazed out of the window.

"Shit is crazy. First Deion, now this muthafuckin' situation with Perez. I don't trust either of their asses," I mumbled, pouring our wine.

"Bella! Bella, you good?" Nikki shouted. "Who the fuck is Perez, and what type of shit you got going on with him?" she spat.

Letting out a deep sigh, I said, "Don't worry about it."

"Are you fucking serious, Bella?"

"Yes," I replied calmly. "Hopefully Deion recovers soon."

"Girl, listen. We both need a night out to get fucked up."

"How is Friday sounding?"

"Yes," Nikki said as she started gathering her things. "If you need anything, call me, girl," she said as she headed out the door.

"I will," I replied, locking up behind her.

My phone started to ring. *Who the hell is this?* I thought as I picked the phone up from the coffee table. Not recognizing the number, I answered on the third ring.

"Hello." No one responded. "Hello?" I repeated.

Heavy breathing started, and I hung up immediately. *What in the hell is going on?* I thought, looking over at my kids. I was getting a feeling like somebody was watching me.

Walking over to the window, I closed the blinds. I sat down on the couch and started playing with Jhai, who was in his car seat. I watched Junior play with his trucks as he watched *Blue's Clues*. The thing that was most important in this whole situation was right in front of me. I knew in my mind I had already left Deion. The betrayal I felt was unmatched. I had to start preparing myself.

Picking up my phone, I called Ma. She answered on the second ring.

"Hello, daughter. What's going on?"

"I'm going to leave him, Ma."

"Who are you talking about?"

"Deion. I know he's cheating, Ma."

"Well, I need you to think about them kids before you make a decision like that."

"Are you joking, Ma? I just told you he was cheating on me."

"I'm just saying, sweetie. Think about it, that's all."

"Whatever. I gotta go, Ma. I have to get the kids ready for bed. I will talk to you later. Bye."

"Bye, Bella. I love you," she said, hanging up.

Chapter 18

Waking up early the following day, I lay in bed with my mind racing with questions. My instincts urged me to investigate before jumping to conclusions. Determined, I began some research, looking into Perez's background. Considering his character, I figured he must have some skeletons in his closet. I started by googling his last name, but nothing substantial came up. Then, recalling that I had his card, I rolled up my sleeves and got to work.

Adrenaline pumping through my veins, I hurried downstairs. Finding his card on the counter, I rushed back upstairs to my computer. Entering his full name, Raymose Perez, into the search, I expanded the query to the surrounding areas. Bingo! An article popped up that matched his name. As I started reading, my immediate thought was, "This guy ain't shit."

> *Officer Raymose Perez, 45, a member of the narcotics squad, was involved in a drug bust gone wrong. Officer Perez has been placed on desk duty in the shooting investigation for the death of Marcus Morton, 21, from Rochester, New York.*

"OMG, this can't be real," I whispered as panic set in. The next thing I did was look up the guy he shot. He had previous encounters with the Rochester PD a few years back; then there was nothing until his death.

"This is serious," I said as I wrote down all Marcus's information and continued searching.

Reaching for my phone, I called Kitty. "Hello, Kitty. Good morning. Can you keep the boys? I have to go see Deion, and Nikki wants to take me out."

"Yes, Bella, that's fine. What time are you thinking about coming?"

"I was going to bring them after we get dressed, like in an hour or so."

"Okay. Bring some Avon too."

"I gotcha, Kitty." I started laughing. Asking for Avon was her way of telling me to bring her some weed.

I got ready first. Then I got the kids together. Going downstairs, I fed them while drinking my coffee, thinking about what I had to do that day and making sure I didn't forget shit.

As I pulled up to Kitty's house, she was already outside. I got out and grabbed the kids as she walked toward us.

"Thank you for watching the kids," I said, handing her the baby before bending down and kissing Junior on his cheeks.

"You're welcome, and tell Deion I said hello."

"Okay, I will. By the way, the Avon is in Jhai's bag," I said, walking out the door.

Jumping into the car, I headed straight to the house to meet Hector. I needed to understand his intentions before going to the hospital. *I want Deion home because I'm not dealing with Perez*, I thought, waiting at a traffic light.

Twenty minutes later, I pulled up to the location. "It's really beautiful with the rose bushes," I remarked, shutting the car door. As I stepped out, I heard my name being called.

"Bella, Bella!"

"Hello, Hector!"

"Come, come, Bella. I have something to show you."

"You sure are full of surprises, but on a serious note, I need to talk to you, Hector."

"Well, go ahead."

"It's Deion," I said as we walked through the foyer toward the living room.

"Don't worry, Bella. I'm the boss for a reason. Now, look at this."

Staring at the bags in front of me, I already knew what it was—a whole load of drugs. I watched as Hector unzipped one of the duffels, pulling out a key of coke.

"This is what makes the world take off its mask, revealing man's true intentions. Bella, it's very powerful, bringing uncertainty amongst friends and family. With great power comes a greater risk."

"Hector, Deion is working with the police, and I think he and Kat have something going on."

"I know."

"What do you mean, you know?" I could feel my body temperature rise. Switching my position, I face him.

"Now you know why I chose you," he said. Bending over to the bag on the left side of him, he lifted up a smaller box. "Turn around, Bella."

I did it with ease, knowing I had made the right decision. "Hector, thank you," I said as I rubbed my fingers across the diamond choker.

"Remember, ain't no money being in your feelings, Bella," he said, cold and calculated.

"You're right," I said, grinning. "I have to go. I still have to go to the hospital. I will keep you posted. And thank you again for everything."

"You're welcome, my sweet Bella."

When I walked into Deion's room at the hospital, I saw him and Rico talking. Standing there in shock, I couldn't believe who I was looking at. *When and how did he get out?* I thought as I smiled.

"How you doin', Bella?" he said, walking over to me with his arms out.

"I'm okay. Just trying to maintain it."

"If you need anything, let me know," Rico said. "All right, y'all. I gotta go. I'll talk to you later, Unc."

"Okay, nephew," Deion said, giving him a head nod.

"Bye." I smiled, excitement filling my soul. *I might need his help, but I'm goin' to wait before I say anything.*

"What's up! How you feelin'?" I asked.

Smiling, Deion looked over at me. "I've missed you. What are you doing here?"

"I need to ask you something. Do you know anything about Perez? I mean anything, like who is he connected to?" I asked, throwing my hands up in desperation.

Deion looked at me with a screwface and folded his arms across his chest. His right knee started bouncing. "Something's wrong with your ears? What are you doing, Bella?"

"What? Nigga, I'm playing chess, not checkers!" I said, not breaking our eye contact.

I knew he was pissed. Placing my right hand on my hip, I said, "Perez was involved in a drug bust gone wrong. Did you know about this? I'm scared, Deion. I don't trust his ass."

He stopped bouncing his knee and uncrossed his arms. "I knew that nigga was trying to set me up," he spat. "Baby, I will never let anything happen to my family. Don't worry. I'll handle it."

I knew he would never let anything happen to us, but his actions had me thinking twice. "I know. So, what are we going to do about Perez, Deion?"

"Don't forget, I get out Monday morning, and I'll handle it."

At that point, I knew to say nothing else about it, so I changed the subject. "Mom and Jake left for California. I miss her already."

"You'll survive, Bella, and she will too."

Looking up at him after his remark, I knew it was time to go. "I have to go handle a few things while Kitty has the kids."

"Okay. How are the kids doing?" he asked.

"They're good. Junior keeps asking where you are, but I just tell him you're on a trip."

"I miss my boys, Bella."

"I'm going out with Nikki tonight."

"Word, okay," he said with disdain. "Be safe."

I glanced back at him, and his words gave me chills. "What is all that for?"

"I just noticed how you've been doin' shit since I've been down," he said, hunching his shoulders.

"Wah?"

"Never mind. Have fun."

Not responding, I rolled my eyes and walked out of his room.

Chapter 19

I started my car and turned up the radio as DMX's "Get at Me, Dog" blazed through the speakers. This song always put me in a crazy state of mind.

"Get at me, dawg," I sang at the top of my lungs, gassing myself up to take this long ride to Rochester. Putting the address in my GPS, I was set to go. Halfway down Route 31, panic arose. I started thinking the worst because my dumb ass didn't take Rico with me. *Thank God it's still daytime.* I thought as I exited the highway.

A nervous energy shot through my body as I got closer to my destination. It was too late to turn around. I was less than three minutes away. "Fuck! You got this, bitch," I yelled, hyping myself up as I pulled in front of 514 Remington Street.

I quickly sized up the young dude in his late twenties sitting on the porch, smoking a blunt. His hair was half braided, and the other half was a dry-looking afro. I was very uncomfortable getting out, walking just close enough.

I said, "Hello."

"Sup, ma?" He smiled.

"Do you know Marcus Morton?"

Instantly, his composure changed as I watched him hit his blunt again. Adjusting his body, he leaned forward, blowing out the smoke as his face hardened. With a cold stare, he said, "Who is asking?"

"I just had a couple of questions to ask about someone connected to his death."

"Why are you asking questions about Marcus?" He paused, gazing at me for a minute before speaking again. "What's your question, miss?"

"Do you know Officer Raymose Perez?"

His whole body tensed up quickly as he cleared his throat. Inhaling another long drag off his blunt before blowing out the smoke, he looked at me and said, "What are you asking about that nigga for? That's a very dangerous man, ma."

My blood pressure rose as my legs weakened. Turning around quickly, I walked back to my car as his chuckles echoed around us.

"Fuck you," I said, getting back inside of my car. My chest pounded as I started crying.

Pulling off, I sent a text to Hector.

Bella: Can we meet?

Hector: Meet me at the warehouse.

Bella: Send me the address. I need an hour if that's still okay with you.

Hector: 64578 Mills Street. That's fine.

Pulling into the nearest gas station, I took a few minutes to think. I was startled by my phone. Nikki's name appeared on the screen.

"Damn," I said before answering.

"What's up, bitttccch? You excited about tonight?"

"Yes," I said as my voice cracked slightly.

"Where are you, Bella?"

"I'm on my way back from Rochester. I had to handle something."

"Girl, you better be careful."

"I know. I'll hit you up as soon as I get into town."

Forty minutes into the ride home, I was close to Medina's drive-in when I saw red and blue lights flashing behind me. I was driving the speed limit. I had no clue why I was getting pulled over. Looking in the rearview mirror, I watched Perez casually step out of his vehicle. Adjusting his vest, he walked toward me. I tugged on my seatbelt as he approached my window, knocking on the glass. Cracking it just enough, my eyes met his. Not showing any fear, I gave Perez the dirtiest look before speaking.

"Is there a problem, officer?"

"Miss Goins, I hear you've been around my old neighborhood."

"I don't know what the fuck you talkin' about."

"This is your only warning." His tone was stern as a crease formed across his forehead. A thick vein popped out the right side of his temple as his eyes narrowed.

Cutting my eyes at him, I rolled up my window and hit the gas. My anxiety instantly kicked in. *How the fuck did he know I was out there?*

As I drove down a graveled road, my dimly lit headlights guided me through the darkness. My tires rumbled over the road. I drove for about twenty miles before the ride was smooth. As I approached a thick barbed wire gate, I called Hector.

"Hello, Hector. I'm pulling in."

"Okay, love."

After I hung up, the gate instantly opened, and a man waved me in. Pulling into the parking lot, I saw Hector emerge from the side of the building with five men by his side. As they walked toward me, I parked my car and stepped out.

"Hello, Hector," I said, extending my hand to him.

Taking my hand, he kissed the top of it before guiding me inside.

"Have a seat, Bella. What's going on? You look bothered."

I looked him in his eyes. "I have to tell you something, and I'm not sure how."

"Just say it."

"There's this officer, Perez, that Deion has been working with, and now they want me to work for him as well."

His body language changed as he put his fingers on his chin. I watched as he spoke with confidence.

"You said Perez?"

"Yes."

Walking closer toward me, Hector smiled as he touched my hair.

"You did a good thing here, Bella."

"I did? What about Perez?"

"I will take care of that."

"One last question," I said, standing up facing him. "Is there a new drop-off location?"

"No. Why would you ask me that?"

"No reason," I said as I walked out the door, not looking back.

Pulling up to the house, I checked my surroundings as I got out. I quickly went inside, sliding down the door as I just sat there against it for a moment, trying to regulate my breathing. Reaching into my bag, I pulled out my phone to call Deion. The phone rang twice before he answered.

"'Sup, Bella? I thought you were going out."

"I am, but a quick question. Where is the new location again?"

There was silence on the other end. I knew that meant I had struck a nerve.

"Why?"

Now I went silent, taking a brief moment before I said, "Your friend Perez stopped me."

"Stopped you? I told you I would handle this when I get out," Deion said, his voice now filled with rage. "You're fucking hardheaded, Bella. You need to learn how to—"

I hung up before he could even finish his sentence. I refused to argue with Deion since he was the one who put us in this position in the first place.

I called Kitty to check on the boys before getting in the shower. As the water ran over my body, my thoughts instantly went to Tyrell as his words devoured my soul.

I'm killing that muthafucka, I thought as I stepped out of the shower.

I felt refreshed and calm after my shower. The radio was blazing through the house as I lotioned up and got dressed. Looking at myself in the mirror, I heard my phone ring. It was Nikki.

"Hey girl, what's up?"

"I'm leaving now. Are you about ready?"

"Let me finish up. Leave in about fifteen minutes, coo'?"

"Okay, hurry up, bitch!"

"Whatever," I said.

Throwing on a pair of cute dark blue fitted jeans with the matching jean jacket that captured all my curves, I topped it off with my new thigh-high boots.

"Okkkaayy, biiittccch." I smiled, modeling in the mirror.

Beep! Beep!

"Hell naw, I know that's not Nikki already," I spat. Opening the window, I screamed, "Give me five minutes, Nikki." Closing the window and making sure it was locked, I finished up. I grabbed my purse, keys and lock up the house.

She was right in the driveway, so I didn't have to walk far. Getting in the car, I said, "Why are you rushing? It ain't even twelve yet." I put on my seatbelt.

"I have to stop by the store first to get a chaser to go with this bottle of Ketel One," Nikki said as she pulled out of the driveway.

"We gettin' turnt up tonight, huh, cuz?"

"Bella, it's been crazy lately. I think we could both use a drink."

"Shid, I agree."

She pulled into the corner store parking lot. "Hurry up, girl. Shit can jump off at any time with all these niggas out here," I said as she parked the car before running inside the store.

Leaning back in my seat just a little, I rolled up. When I heard loud music from a car at the light, it caught my attention. Turning my head to look, I saw Tyrell.

You can't be fucking serious, I thought, squinting my eyes to make sure. *This nigga switched whips.* I slid into the driver's seat to follow him. Staying two cars behind him, I hit every turn he made.

I'm on your ass, muthafucka.

Startled by my phone, I saw Nikki's name appear on my screen. I quickly answered.

"Where the fuck are you, Bella? Bring me my car."

"Nikki, give me a second. I forgot something," I said, hanging up. I threw my phone in the other seat, still keeping Tyrell in my sight. I couldn't risk not knowing where this nigga was going. All I needed was an opportunity.

We hit a couple of lefts, then a right or two until we ended in lower town on Van Buren Street. I acted as if I was driving by, watching through my rearview mirror to see where he was going. As he walked across the street, I pulled into the nearest driveway, turning around to face him. Shutting off my lights, I watched as he walked into this white house with black shutters that sat on the corner.

"Fuck, I finally found his ass." Wiping the sweat off my forehead, I felt relief. Smiling as I turned my lights back on, I headed back to pick up Nikki.

Chapter 20

Entering the room, I caught sight of Deion and Perez engaged in conversation. Deion wore a smirk that immediately raised my suspicions. What in the hell were they discussing? The energy in the room shifted as they both glanced at me, abruptly ending their discussion. Despite the uneasy vibe, I walked in with a smile, determined to navigate the unknown territory that seemed to be unfolding.

"Hi, Bella, whatcha doing here?"

"I wanted to come to see you. Is that cool with you?"

"Bella, we meet again." Perez nodded at me.

"Ummmm, yeah." I smiled. "What's up with you, Deion?"

"Nothing. You okay?" he asked, looking at me strangely.

"Yeah, I'm good. Y'all sure are friendly lately," I said, smacking my lips.

"He just came up here to check on my status."

Perez interrupted. "I'll come see you later, Deion. Now, don't forget to let me know."

"A'ight," Deion said as Perez walked out the door, smiling.

I looked at Deion with a death stare once Perez was out of the room. "What the fuck is wrong wit' you, nigga?"

"Don't worry so much. I got us."

"Whatever," I said, looking down at my phone as I received a text from a number I had never seen before.

Unknown: I miss you

Bella:??

Unknown: I need to see you.

Bella: Who is this?

Unknown: Tyrell

Bella: How did you get my number?

Unknown: I will explain everything when I see you.

Deion knew I was distracted, but I didn't give a fuck. I couldn't tell him what was going on.

"I'm about to go. I have to pick up the kids from Kitty," I told him.

"Seems like something important came up."

"I'll see you tomorrow. The kids will be so happy to see you."

Pulling out of the hospital parking lot, I looked down at my phone and saw another text from Tyrell.

Tyrell: You still meeting me?

Bella: Where you stay at?

Tyrell: 13 Van Buren the white house on the corner

Damn, I was right. A leopard never changes his spots!

Bella: Let me get the kids settled, and I will come through.

I called Nikki and asked her to pick up the kids from Kitty's, and she agreed. I headed home to jump in the shower and get dressed. As I finished my hair, my phone rang. My mom's name appeared on the screen.

"Mom? Mom? Are you okay?"

All I heard was crying as she tried to catch her breath. I lowered my voice because I became scared at this point.

"Mom, talk to me." I swear I don't know why, but I also started crying with her. I could hear my mom trying to pull herself together. "It's okay, whatever it is."

"Bella, Jake stabbed someone, and he's in jail."

"What!" I went silent for a moment. "Mom, stop playing." I started getting nervous, and my heart started palpitating faster.

"I'm not playing." She started crying harder.

"Mom, tell me what happened."

"I don't know what happened. I wasn't there. I was told he just stabbed a man at the bar, and the guy was hurt."

"What the fuck?" She was devastated. I could hear it all in her voice. "Find out more details and call me back, Mom."

"Okay, baby, I love you," she said before hanging up.

"What in the hell is going on?" I yelled. *This shit is crazy,* I thought, pulling out the lingerie I was going to wear. I proceeded to lotion every part of my body. I decided to wear this cute little back-open, pussy-out, easy-access teddy that made my breasts pop. I put on some fishnet thigh-high stockings and grabbed my red bottom heels, which were his favorite.

Another text came through from Tyrell. *This nigga must have ESP,* I thought.

Tyrell: Where you at?

Bella: I am getting ready to chill.

I cocked it back, put one in the chamber, and put it in my purse. Hurrying to slip on my heels, I misted my body with Versace Yellow Diamond perfume before picking up my black trench coat. I gave myself one last look before grabbing my keys. I walked out of the house.

Chapter 21

Walking into Tyrell's house, a rush of anger hit the core of my soul. The vibe between us was off as we stood there, in an awkward position, trying to feel each other out.

"What's good, Bella?"

I nodded slightly as the sound of his voice reminded me of that cold metal up against my golden skin. I knew at this moment I was about to do something so sinister that a chill ran throughout my body. Clearing the lump out of my throat, I stepped back slightly with a fake smile.

"Was it personal?" I asked.

His silence was unsettling as I watched Tyrell's body shift. With hesitation, he spoke. "Bella, I can explain."

"Just tell me why?" I whispered, lowering my head. "We have so much history. I don't understand, Tyrell."

Grabbing his glass of brown liquor off the coffee table, he took a swig as his face softened. "I know I fucked up. I'll do whatever I have to do to make it right. Can we take this conversation to the bedroom?"

Oh, he thinks shit is sweet. I smirked. "Naw, ain't no need to. You can explain that shit right here."

"Follow me, please. I can show you better than I can tell you, Bella."

Clutching my purse, I agreed. As we walked down the hallway, I saw red and pink rose petals creating a path to the room. *Oh, this nigga trying to have a real special moment,* I thought, noticing the flickering lights on the wall.

Grabbing my left hand, Tyrell guided me into the room.

"This is so fucking sweet," I whispered as a smile appeared on my face.

"I thought this might make it up to you, Bella."

"Not even close, but good try. Lay the fuck down," I said, forcibly pushing him back on the bed. I placed my purse on his black nightstand. "You ready to make this shit up to me?"

"Whatever it takes," he said, rubbing his hands together as he licked his lips.

Allowing my trench coat to fall to the floor, I got on the bed, towering over him, spreading my legs like the Red Sea. I lowered myself onto his face. *I hope this nigga enjoys his last supper,* I thought, allowing him to feast on my pussy.

"Umm uhh . . . fuck," I moaned, thrusting my hips back and forth. *I can't enjoy this nigga, can I?* I thought. Tears started falling down my cheeks as my legs began to shake. I tightened my grip around the metal headboard as my juices released from my body.

"You missed this pussy, didn't you?" I asked, moving back to position myself over his dick. Spitting on the head before placing it deep into my throat, I slowly bobbed my head up and down.

"Ahh ahh," he moaned, grabbing my waist and pulling me closer. The look in his eyes let me know he wanted to fill my body with every inch of his dick.

Rotating my hips in a circular motion, I rode him fast and furious, using his chest as support. Licking my lips, I leaned back as Tyrell felt my breasts.

"You sexy as hell, Bella. Ride this muthafuckin' dick," he whispered, biting his bottom lip. "You gon' cum for daddy?"

"Yess . . . ahhh," I moaned, lowering my body closer to him as I slid my hand in my purse, pulling out my pistol. Lifting myself back up, I pointed the pistol dead in between his eyes, allowing the cold iron to touch his temple.

"Oh, shit!" he said as his eyes got big. "Bitch, did you lose your fucking mind?" he said as I was raised my arm. I swung with force and slammed the butt of the pistol across his face.

"How the fuck does that feel, nigga? I don't recommend yo' ass moves."

"Bella! Bella! You don't understand," he pleaded as blood dripped down the side of his face.

"Understand? Did you think I was about to let you slide?" I said, continuing to point the gun in his face.

Tyrell was about to start speaking when I saw a flash from the corner of my eye. Seconds later, blood and chunks splattered all over my face. I touched my face as panic set in. Jumping off Tyrell's limp body, I screamed. Blood was everywhere. Suddenly, I heard a voice behind me that made me crumble to the floor.

"Now, Bella, stop screaming. It's only blood."

Damnit, it couldn't be him. Fuck! I thought, twisting around with the pistol still in my hand.

"Back the fuck up now," I said.

"Young lady, you look like you're in enough trouble, and you need some help."

"Why? I didn't do it."

"If you never pulled a trigger before, you could have never dealt with the aftermath," he said, walking over to me. He rubbed his fingers softly down my face.

Taking the pistol out of my hands, Perez began to wipe it down. I mumbled, "Thank you."

"Hector must like you," he said. "Now, go wash up and get out of here. Miss Goins, make sure you burn everything you have on, including those nice pumps. Now, get moving."

"Okay." I watched as Perez pulled out his phone. I listened as he said, "The job is done. Send the cleaners in."

I just stared at him as he handed me the gun back. I didn't respond. I turned and walked off straight to the bathroom. Turning on the hot water, I scanned the room. I had no time to panic. I grabbed the first towel I saw on the edge of the tub, neatly placed next to a glass of wine. I washed up briefly and got dressed.

"I'll be getting a hold of you," Perez said in a stern voice.

Smacking my lips, I said, "Whatever."

Walking out the door, I instantly took off running to the bridge, throwing the gun over before getting into my car.

Thirty minutes later, I pulled into our driveway. Walking to the back of the house, I stripped my clothes off before unlocking the door. Immediately grabbing a small plastic bag sitting on top of the washer, I threw my clothes in it.

Rushing up the stairs, I hit the shower first, still trying to process what had happened. Washing my face, sobbing uncontrollably, I was determined to scrub every inch of my body. When I got out of the shower, my phone rang back-to-back. Deion's name appeared. Why was he calling?

"Hello, Deion."

"What are you doing?" he asked.

"Shit, just getting out of the shower. Let me call you back. I have to finish drying off and get dressed."

"A'ight, I love you."

"Whatever, bye."

I know I need to burn them muthafuckin' clothes, I thought as a nervous sensation shot through my body. Jumping up, I walked back downstairs. I grabbed the matches along with a couple of logs to light the fire. I watched the amber flames spread before walking back to pick up the plastic bag from the laundry room.

Returning to the fire, I tossed the bag in, watching as it disintegrated before my eyes along with Tyrell. I had so many questions. *How do all these pieces connect Perez with Hector? How long have they been working together? Does the dummy know?*

Afterward, I went to lie down in bed, processing all that had happened that night. I kept hearing Perez's voice in my head, repeating Hector's name and the fact that he would be getting a hold of me. What could Perez possibly want with me?

I'm giving Hector a piece of my mind, I thought and immediately sent him a text.

Bella: So you knew about Perez the whole time?

Hector: He works for me.

Hector: I need you to do me a favor, can you?

Bella: ??

Hector: I need you not to mention this to anyone, not even Deion. I have a leak. I'm trying to catch.

Bella: Okay.

Waking up, I was startled by my phone vibrating repeatedly. It was Deion.

"Where are you?" he asked.

"Good morning to you as well," I said, clearing my throat. "I overslept. Give me twenty minutes."

"Okay. Can you grab my black Champion sweatsuit with my black Air Force Ones?"

"Yeah, I'll see you shortly."

Gathering his shit, I put everything in his duffel bag. I went to the bathroom to wash my face and brush my teeth. Staring in a mirror for a while, I started questioning myself. *Did that shit happen last night?* After drying my face, I told myself there was nothing I could do for Tyrell. I was going to kill him anyway. But the real question was, why was Perez there, and why would Hector have not mentioned it to me?

I desperately needed to get a cup of coffee before I went to pick up Deion. I finished getting ready and headed out the door.

I told myself I would no longer think of Tyrell and would try to somehow make it work with Deion's cheating ass. I just couldn't get past the fact that he and Perez were working together, and now knowing Hector had secrets. We both had to come to some sort of understanding if we wanted to outsmart Perez.

I pulled up to the emergency room parking lot, figuring we wouldn't be long since he was already checked out and dressed. I was tired of coming up here.

As I got to the door of Deion's room, I saw he had a big smile on his face when he greeted me. I fake smiled as I walked up to him, hugging him.

"Is everything okay, Bella?"

"It's perfect now," I said sarcastically.

I helped Deion put his clothes on. As he stood to pull his sweats up, the nurse walked in. Handing me his paperwork, she told him, "You need to take it easy. We have made a follow-up appointment with your doctor. You need to keep this appointment for your aftercare."

"Yes, ma'am, thank you," Deion responded.

As I pushed Deion down the main hallway past the nurse's station, the attending staff said their goodbyes, wishing him well. Leaving Deion with the nurse at the automatic doors, I went to get the car.

I'm ready to handle this with my man, I told myself. Not fully aware of what was coming next, I was just happy Deion was coming home.

As he got in the car, I asked, "Is there any place you'd like to go?"

"Home, baby."

"Home it is."

Reaching over in the ashtray, I handed him the Dutch I rolled before I came to pick him up. Deion looked over at me, smiling as he tried to lean over as far as he could, putting his lips up in the air for me to kiss them. I drove off as Deion sparked the blunt, and I turned the radio up a little bit more, hearing "Unpredictable," that joint by Jamie Foxx and Luda. I can't even lie. This shit was dope.

We drove for a while, not saying a word to each other, just caught up in the moment. It was nice.

I pulled up to the house just as Deion finished the blunt.

"There are those fucking lights, Deion. It is probably your friend."

Anger came across Deion's face as he glared in the mirror, looking at Perez.

"This shit is getting out of hand for real, Deion."

"Yeah, you're right. It's out of control." He watched him walk up to the driver's side of the car. I rolled down the window before he approached. Looking back at Deion, I got pissed.

"This is the shit I am talking about. What does he want?" I asked.

"Shit, I don't know, but we are about to find out."

Perez leaned on the door, telling us to follow him. He laughed as he spun around to walk back to his car.

"You are so fucking stupid. Look at this bullshit you got us in. What the fuck is wrong with you?"

He could not respond.

Perez pulled up next to us, staring at us for a second before pulling off.

Shaking my head, I said, "Deion, your dumb ass just got out of the hospital, and we're already in some shit." I pulled off, following Perez.

"Calm down and shut the fuck up, Bella. We only need to hear what he has to say. I need to know how to move around him."

Rolling my eyes, I said, "How stupid do you think I am? You don't know how smart Perez is, do you?"

Glaring at me, he said, "Who's sounding crazy now, Bella?" His tone was deep with conviction as he spoke.

Perez turned down this narrow dirt road. I turned as well, continuing to follow him for a little bit further when I realized this was where Hector and I met. He shut off his car and got out, walking to the door. I threw the car in park, waiting a minute before shutting off my car. I contemplated if I should just leave.

Perez waved, signaling us to get out. I was nervous. Shit, we both were.

As we walked in, I noticed there wasn't as much light as when I came here with Hector. Looking around, I saw four crates that sat back a little bit, followed by a card table that only had three chairs.

"Sit the fuck down," Perez said. "By now, we all know I'm a man down."

"That's not our problem," Deion said.

"Well, it sorta is," Perez said, his voice filled with sarcasm.

I almost passed out! *I know he's not talking about Tyrell. Holy shit!*

"Tyrell was killed last night. Bella, do you have additional information to add?"

"Why would I?"

"Are you on board?"

Disappointed, I nodded yes. Deion looked at me weirdly but didn't say anything.

Perez walks over to one of those crates, grabbing a crowbar that sat on top of it. He then opened the crate, pulling out ten keys of coke, one at a time.

My eyes got big as I started breathing heavily. *It has the same marking on the product Hector had. Is this the leak?* I thought.

"That is a lot of coke," I said, watching as he placed them on the table.

Deion looked at me. "Bella, are you sure we can handle this?"

"Fuck no!"

I looked over at Perez. The heat coming from his direction was heavy.

Not breaking eye contact, he smirked. "You have no choice."

Looking over at Deion, I shrugged. "Let's get this money," I told him.

"Word, Bella," Deion agreed.

Perez started laughing as he threw the coke in a duffel bag.

"This won't take long," Deion said as Perez tossed the duffel bag in my direction.

"What the fuck, Perez?" I said.

Grabbing the bag, I walked away. Deion followed me to the car. That ride home was quiet—no radio, no nothing. I was pissed and had nothing to say.

When we got home, I noticed Deion was hurting and struggling to get out of the car.

"Hold on, Deion. I am coming. Just let me grab these bags really quick."

"I'm ready to go inside."

"Shit, me too."

Grabbing the bags and his crutches, I walked to Deion as he sat at the edge of the seat, waiting for me. I handed him his crutches and stood in front of him so he could catch his balance. He started walking. I followed behind him until we reached the door. Setting the bags on the porch, I unlocked the door and helped him to the couch.

"Do you need anything?"

"Yeah, can you hand me the hospital bag and grab me a bottle of water?"

"Okay."

Walking in the kitchen, I grabbed both bags, then the water, and brought them back to him.

"I am about to hop in the shower. You good?"

"Yeah."

Deion reached in his bag, grabbing his pain medicine. I watched as he raised the bottle to his lips, dumping the pills in his mouth like a pro, followed by the bottle of water I handed him. Still standing there, I shook my head in disbelief.

"You sure you're good?"

"Nah, I ain't."

"What?"

"What was all that about back there?"

"Nigga, you trippin'."

"A'ight, Bella."

Walking off, I went upstairs to the room. *Fuck this nigga! It's his fault we're in this mess in the first place,* I thought as I lit up a blunt.

Chapter 22

Turning on the radio before I jumped in the shower, I cried as the water ran down my body. Sobbing in my hands, I suddenly felt his touch.

"I love you, Bella. I'm sorry, baby, about everything. I could not risk losing my family. You are everything to me."

I did not respond. He must have forgotten, but I had not. I knew he was still fucking Kat.

"How did we get here, Deion?"

There was no response. Pushing my hair back, he leaned in, kissing my neck. "We're gonna be okay, baby."

"You think so?" I said, smacking my lips.

I got out of the shower. Deion grabbed my hand, leading me straight into our bedroom.

"Lay down on the bed. You miss daddy?"

"You know I missed you."

As he placed kisses on my inner thigh, I reached over to the nightstand. I grabbed the blunt, lighting it before I closed my eyes, inhaling deeply. Deion spread my legs further apart, licking his way up to my pretty pussy. He slid two fingers inside of me as he spit on my clit. Moaning, I dropped my head back, smiling.

"Ahh! This feels so good." I wrapped my hands around his head, guiding him as he sucked my juices aggressively. A tingly sensation ran through my body. "Ugh, yes! Yes, don't you stop." Instantly, my body went into convulsions, shaking as I released my juices.

I giggled as Deion stood up, stumbling as he wiped his mouth with the back of his hand before smacking me on my thigh.

"Flip the fuck over," he said in a demanding tone.

"Oooh, yes! Talk your shit."

Rolling over on my stomach, I eased up on my knees, slowly scooting back to the edge of the bed with my ass in the air. Arching my back automatically, Deion grabbed my hips as he eased inside of me. I gasped.

"You missed this dick, didn't you, bitch?"

I didn't respond. He grabbed my hair, yanking my head back as he fucked me harder, sliding further inside of me.

"Ugh! Ahh!" I moaned. My eyes rolled back slightly as I turned my head, looking back at Deion, feeling every bit of him inside of me. "Fuck me!" I repeatedly yelled as his stroke game became more aggressive. "Deion, oooh. Tell me you love this sweet pussy."

"You know I do. This my pussy. I will never let it go," he said, wrapping his hand around my neck, tightening his grip with every stroke he made, making sure I would never forget.

Maybe it was the medication he took, but he was fucking me as if I was Keisha from the movie *Belly*. He kept reminding me this was his pussy as he busted inside me.

After we finished, he sat on the edge of the bed. "Light that blunt back up, Bella."

Rolling over, I grabbed the blunt and lit it as he started talking about how we were about to blow up in the dope game. Reminiscing on how things used to be, I hit the blunt, blowing out the smoke.

"Yeah, we are, huh," I said, passing the blunt to him.

"Bella, I will get us a team together, some of our closest friends and family. All you must do is keep track of who has what and who owes. We can run this like a Fortune 500 company. What do you think?"

"Maybe," I said. "I never thought about it this deep. We only hustle for us. This is a whole new level now, Deion. Have you thought about that?"

"It's not that big of a deal. We just keep moving like we always do."

"Yeah, whatever. We are also dealing with a dirty cop and Hector."

"You don't seem confident."

"I'm not, Deion."

"Just hear me out before you throw in the towel. We have all the cards we need to play this game. We have information nobody does, like raids, wiretaps, indictments, sealed and unsealed. We know who is working with the people."

I said, "You cannot be serious, Deion. You are working with the boys."

"Bella, you know what I mean."

I didn't say shit after that. Rolling over, I went to sleep.

Chapter 23

The next morning, I awoke a bit earlier than usual. Shifting in bed, I glanced over to check if Deion was still asleep, and indeed, he was. As I stared at him, a mix of confusion and anger swirled within me. The toll of my involvement with him and the dangerous world of drugs had cost me so much. It felt like everything had been stolen from me.

Deciding to take a moment to check up on my mom, I picked up my phone and dialed her number.

"Hi, Mom."

"Hey, baby. How are my grandchildren?"

"They are good, Ma. How are you doing? Do you feel any better?"

"I'm okay, baby."

I could tell by my mom's voice that she wasn't the same. I just listened as she started speaking.

"Jake finally left the county and went upstate. His family has been extremely nice, helping me. But I do miss you and the kids. You should come out here."

"Soon. I will be out there soon. I love you, but I gotta handle something."

"Bye, baby. I'll talk to you later."

When we went to see Kitty later, she noticed my vibe had changed. "Hey, Bella, you think I could keep the kids just one more night?"

I turned to look at Deion for his decision.

"Yeah, it's coo', Kitty. They can go," Deion said.

"You sure want to take them, Kitty?" I asked.

"Yes, I'm sure."

"Thanks, sis." Getting up, I grabbed the boys' bags to replenish what they had already used. Once I was done, I zipped the bags and set them down, picking up Junior and giving him hugs and kisses before I did the same for Jhai.

"Okay, I guess we are about to roll out."

"Deion, can I get some Avon?" Kitty asked.

"Yeah, sis, take this," he said, handing her a plastic bag full. "This a month's worth of free babysitting."

"Little bro," Kitty said. We all started to laugh.

"You're welcome, Kitty," Deion said as I shut the door.

Within three days, the product was gone. The rapid turnover didn't surprise me. It moved quickly because it was top-notch. We were offering it at a more competitive price than any of our rivals. The outlook was positive, and the profits were climbing. Fortunately, the Perez situation wasn't posing a problem.

My primary concern revolved around Deion. It seemed like he wasn't fully grasping the gravity of our current situation. The fact that he hadn't mentioned Perez to Hector yet was baffling. I attempted to bring it up with him a few times, but he consistently brushed it off. He seemed to be navigating a perilous game, underestimating the potential risks associated with both Perez and Hector. That alone sent shivers down my spine.

Speaking of Hector, I decided to send him a text.

Bella: Hey.

Hector: Is everything okay?

Bella: Yes, can we meet?

Hector: I am at the Best Western, room 236. Can you be here in thirty minutes?

Bella: Okay, see you soon.

The impact this man has had on my life was nothing short of a blessing. I feel a deep sense of loyalty toward him, almost like I owed it to him. In fact, he deserved it.

Getting up, I needed to create an excuse for Deion to leave. It was unsettling how these lies were piling up, and I was starting to scare myself.

Walking into the living room, I found Deion staring out the window.

"Deion, you okay?"

"Yeah."

"I have to go handle something with Sammy real quick."

"Okay, be safe and tell Sammy he should come by real soon. We have to catch up like the ole days."

"Yeah, I will mention it to him," I said before going back upstairs.

I could not get super cute. That would throw Deion off. I just kept on the regular shit I had, until I could make a quick stop at the Tim Hortons to change. Grabbing my keys and my purse, I left.

Chapter 24

A few days later, Deion strolled into the house with a beaming smile and positive vibes. I'd describe it as arrogant, but who was I to judge?

"We're hosting a party, Bella."

"Why?" I inquired.

"It's been a while since we've done anything. Can't we splurge a bit with this money?"

"Whatever, it's your call. You do seem unusually cheerful. Where have you been?"

"Don't start, Bella. Can't a brother just be in a good mood?"

I rolled my eyes, choosing not to respond. Leaning over the baby, I reached for my phone to dial Nikki.

"What's up? What are you up to?" she asked.

"Your cousin is in high spirits and wants to throw a party. I've got some smoke and wine. Come through."

"Okay, just give me a minute."

"Bet," I said. After ending the call with Nikki, I dove into the search for venues. Buffalo had a few options, though some seemed subpar according to the reviews. As I scrolled further, I stumbled upon a promising spot called The Ballroom and decided to give them a ring.

"The Ballroom. This is Sincere. How can I assist you?"

"Hello, I'm interested in renting out your establishment."

"What's your vision?" he asked.

I laid out my plans and mentioned that I'd swing by to check out the venue. Once Nikki arrived at the house, I grabbed my keys, and we hit the road.

"So, we're throwing a party, Bella?"

"Yeah, girl. Deion is in the mood to splurge. I found a spot called The Ballroom in Buffalo."

"Oh, nice choice. What's the game plan?"

"I'm thinking an open bar with some grub, and maybe spruce it up with a few decorations. Is that going overboard, Nikki?"

"Naw, I don't think so. You do know Shay caters, right?"

"Ooh, yeah! I forgot," I said as we headed toward I-90.

We drove in silence for a short while until Nikki turned on the radio. I did not know what song was playing, but it triggered something inside me, causing me to break down crying.

"Bella, what's wrong? Please pull over."

I pulled off to the side of the road. All of my emotions were released at one time. I was so upset that I started heaving. It felt like I couldn't breathe as tears continued to fall.

"What's wrong? Why are you crying?"

"I can't take it anymore. Me and the kids are leaving."

"What! Where are you going? Why are you leaving? When?"

"Deion has lost his mind. I can't do this shit anymore, cuz. I'm leaving after the party."

Nikki's eyes began to swell as she looked at me in shock. I started to cry with her, feeling like I let my best friend down.

Clearing my throat before speaking, I wiped my eyes and said, "I'm sorry, Nikki."

"Bella, it's going to be okay," she said, looking in the mirror, wiping her face.

After I pulled myself together, we got back on the road. We drove in silence. I exited the freeway for Galleria Mall.

"Bella, I'll be here for you and the kids," Nikki said.

"I know."

"Fuck this shit right now. We're going shopping on Deion's dime," she said with a smile.

Pulling into the mall, I parked and shut the car off before getting out. "I have no clue what I'm going to wear, but I do know what Deion likes. All white with some stilettos."

"You so stupid, bitch. Let's go in here and look around."

Walking into the mall, she pointed at the first store she saw. "Let's look around in this store."

As we walked around the store, I didn't see anything I liked, but Nikki found a couple of things. She walked into the dressing room to try on her outfits. Hanging around, I was thinking about Hector and Deion. I was distracted. As I walked back toward the dressing room, Nikki stepped out, twirling around in this cute-ass mini dress.

"Okay, miss thang."

"This the one. You like it, Bella?"

"That's fire. Now, hurry up. I'm hungry."

Nikki walked back into the dressing room to change. Walking up front, I waited on her. She came up to the counter, and I handed her a stack.

"Thanks, Bella."

"You're welcome."

"Come on, Nikki. Let's go to the food court. I am starving."

As we walked over to the food court, Nikki suggested that we get Greek chicken wraps.

"Oh, that sounds so good," I agreed.

We walked up to the counter, placed our orders, and moved to the side. "This is going to be the bomb, Bella."

"We'll see." I laughed. "You always got me trying different shit."

While I paid for our food, Nikki found us a table. I was praying she didn't ask any more questions because I didn't want to answer them. I hated lying to her, but it had to be done.

We sat down and began to eat. "Okay, you were right. This is the bomb."

"I told you."

"Nikki, I don't want to go home. I hope Deion isn't there."

"You got this, Bella. Don't let him change your morals and what you think is right."

"Easier said than done, I guess."

We finished our food and headed back home. Walking in, I found Deion pacing from the living room to the kitchen, mumbling. Nikki and I looked at each other.

"What the fuck is wrong, Deion?"

"I got this, Bella." Deion stopped dead in his tracks, looking me in my eyes. "Niggas just robbed me."

Nikki and I looked at each other, but quickly my attention was back on Deion. "Tell me exactly what happened."

"All I know is a nigga gotta pay. They don't know who they fucking wit'. I run this shit!" he yelled.

The anger in his voice frightened me. He was so mad. Something snapped in Deion. I was scared, and so was Nikki. Out of nervousness, I grabbed the blunt Deion had rolled up, lighting it.

"Bella, shit was off all fucking day. I stopped by the shop after I did a pickup. Tone was on the phone, but he jumped off too fast when I walked in. I should've gone with my gut."

"Deion, you sound crazy," I said, inhaling the blunt.

"I'm telling you, Tone set me up," he said, punching the palm of his left hand.

"Deion, please, let's think this through."

"Ain't nothing to think about. That nigga is about to die."

"You don't even know if Tone had anything to do with it."

"It doesn't matter."

"We don't need the heat around us, Deion."

He stared right through me. The intensity of his stare scared Nikki, causing her to get up and leave without even saying goodbye. Hell, I thought about following behind her. But instead, I went upstairs. Going over to the dresser to take off my jewelry, looking down, I saw lines of coke just sitting there.

This nigga is tripping now.

"Deionnnnnn, come here!" I screamed.

Running up the steps, Deion stopped at the door, looking at me. "That ain't nothing. I forgot to pick it up."

"Whatcha mean? These are lines, Deion."

"Fuck it. I needed to get right. Why the fuck you questioning me anyways?"

"Whatever, nigga. Are you stupid? Don't you know you never get high on your supply?" Grabbing my jacket, I went downstairs, walking straight out the door.

Driving around, I contemplated what my choices were. Deion was out of control. I knew if I didn't play this right, my life would be on the line. After clearing my head, I finally went home, praying Deion wasn't there. Thank God his whip was gone, giving me time.

All of a sudden, someone started knocking hard as fuck on my door. I was scared.

Who could that be?

Grabbing a wooden bat that sat next to the couch, I picked it up and walked toward the window. Peeking out from behind the blinds, I called out, "Who is it?"

"Bella, it's Officer Perez."

What the hell? I thought. Opening the door, I said, "What do you want? Deion isn't home."

"I know. Can I come in for a minute?"

Opening the door wider, he walked in. I saw he had a stern look on his face.

"Do you know where Deion keeps his coke?" he asked.

"Naw, why?"

"Have you seen anything out of the ordinary?"

"Naw. Where are you going with this? I'm really confused, Perez."

"You need to get rid of anything you shouldn't have in the house."

His words echoed around me as panic set in. "Why? Are we in any kind of trouble?"

"You're okay. It's just for cautionary reasons."

Something didn't seem right to me. "Are we done here?" I said, standing up to signal our conversation was finished.

Perez stood as well and walked toward the door. Stopping in front of it, he turned around and glared at me. "Hector said to call him, Bella," he said, laughing as he opened the door and walked out.

"He knows my number," I said. Locking the door behind him, it felt like the walls were closing in on me, and they were closing fast.

I went into the kitchen and poured myself a shot of Ketel One while calling my mother.

"Hey, Mom, what are you doing?"

"Nothing much. Just writing Jake. What's going on?"

"I was calling to let you know I'm coming with the kids real soon. Are you ready for us?"

"Oooh, baby, yes! When are you leaving?"

"I can't say exactly yet, Mom, but just know soon."

"Okay. I'll start getting things set up for you guys."

Turning my head before I responded, I heard Deion come in. As he walked past me, I saw he was covered in blood.

"Shit, let me call you back, Mom."

He started taking off his clothes and putting them in a plastic bag. After tying it up, he threw it at me.

"Burn this shit."

I didn't ask any questions. I knew he had already done something horrific. Walking to the fireplace, I put a couple of logs in, followed by a match. I waited until the amber flames were consistent, then threw the plastic bag in the fire. *The shit you do for a man you love.* I watched it burn, along with his secrets. This couldn't be a coincidence. First, Perez told me to burn my shit, now Deion.

Chapter 25

"Did you get rid of it?" Deion spat into the phone. As I overheard his conversation, I intentionally made some noise entering the room. I didn't want to escalate his anxiety any further. Deion hung up immediately. Without uttering a word, he started pacing back and forth, rubbing his head.

"Baby, relax. I need you to pull it together. I'll go run you a shower."

"I don't need a shower right now."

"Whatever." I rolled my eyes at him. "Fuck you too."

Sitting on the side of the bed, I started rolling up the smoke on my stand. *What the fuck is wrong with this nigga? He is way out of control.*

I watched as he sniffed two lines of coke before exiting the room.

"Shut the door behind you, Deion," I yelled.

Grabbing the edge of the door, he slammed it shut.

"That was unnecessary," I screamed.

Lying in bed, I just could not believe this was our new normal.

That early sunrise was always beautiful. Thanking God for another day, I just lay there for a while as the smell of food hit my nose. Sniffing the aroma of eggs and freshly brewed coffee, I smiled as Deion entered the room, carrying breakfast on a tray. It was all right, considering what went down last night.

Taking a sip of coffee, I raised my eyebrows over the cup, looking at him.

"How did you sleep?" he asked.

"I barely slept."

"How is the party coming?"

"I have to go up there today to pay them."

"Okay. I left money on the dresser. It should cover the entire cost."

"Thank you."

"Bella, about last night—"

"Don't, Deion. The club is in Buffalo. It's called The Ballroom. Have you heard of it?"

"I'm sorry, Bella. I know I've been off lately."

That last bite of food was hard to swallow. I had to take another sip of coffee before I started laughing. "Yeah, a little off," I said sarcastically.

That must have pissed him off. "That's your fucking problem. You don't know how to listen to a nigga." Getting up, Deion stomped off.

Picking up my phone, I called Nikki.

"Hey, good morning, Nikki. You're still going with me to check out this venue, right?"

"Yes, I'll ride with you."

"Okay, I'll be there after I get ready. Deion is keeping the boys to make it easier."

"Okay, I'll see you shortly."

It didn't take me that long to get ready. Going downstairs to tell Deion I was leaving, I kissed the kids and left out the door. Pulling up in front of Nikki's apartment, I beeped the horn and turned up the radio just a little. It was Ashanti's "Foolish." I felt that joint right there. My favorite part came on, so I started rocking out, singing, "*I love you. I can't deny. I can't see how you could bring me to so many tears after all these years!*" Yes, girl, how could he?

By this time, Nikki was laughing as she got in the car. "I know you are feeling this joint right here," I told her. I continued singing until the song ended, then turned down the radio.

"Nikki, what's the quickest way to Buffalo?"

"Straight down Transit and jump on I-Ninety."

It didn't take us that long, maybe forty minutes or so, and that was with traffic. We pulled up in front of The Ballroom.

"It looks nice on the outside, Nikki."

"Yes, just wait until we go inside."

"I'm super excited to see the inside."

"I think there might be a hookah lounge too, Bella."

Checking myself in the mirror, I applied some lip gloss before shutting the car off. We walked a short distance to the door. We were greeted by this tall, fine-ass brother with light skin, hazel eyes, medium build, and well-groomed facial hair. He was giving off a real grown man vibe. I was feeling his style. Looking at Nikki, I saw she was smiling hard.

The gentleman extended his hand to me. "Hello, my name is Sincere, and I run this establishment. How can I help you, pretty ladies?"

"I called about renting the venue. I'm Bella."

"Right," he said, snapping his fingers. "Welcome. Please follow me."

"I'm sorry, this is my girlfriend, Nikki."

"Nice to meet you, Nikki," he said, winking at her.

"Hello," Nikki said, smiling.

"Follow me, ladies."

I looked around as Sincere was telling us about the services and the amenities that came along with specific packages. I was listening, but something at the bar caught my attention. I spotted Kat.

What the fuck? Why is she here? We made eye contact before I started talking to Sincere.

"That bar is dope," I said. It was in the middle of the club, oval-shaped. It was stocked to the rim on every shelf with all different kinds of liquor and wine. There were eight giant televisions connected to it as well, playing something different on each of them. In the corner was a DJ booth.

"The DJ will be provided in two of the packages," Sincere said.

"Okay," I responded. Looking at the format of the club, I could see it was a very decent size. The VIP section had a hookah setup. I also looked for every exit within range of the sitting lounges, just in case.

"Now that was nice, Nikki."

"I told you, Bella," she said, pointing out the sheer curtains for privacy.

Looking at Nikki, I wondered if she had been here before. I noticed the corners of her mouth curl up as she winked at me. We continued walking toward the back area. On the way, I saw a couple of pool tables and some dartboards hanging on the wall.

"Come on, let me show you the best part about this whole club," Sincere said.

Walking past the bar, I glanced over at Kat. The expression on her face made me nervous as I looked up and saw what she was watching: Channel 4 News. I couldn't hear it, but I saw the banner that came across the television screen in bold letters, **Breaking News from Lockport, New York**. Nikki and I looked at each other as the news anchor was standing in front of Tone's barbershop.

"Can you turn this up, please?"

Kat looks at me as she turned the volume up.

"Thank you," I said.

"A deadly shooting late yesterday evening left two dead and one injured," the news anchor reported.

I froze. I couldn't speak a word.

Looking over at Kat, I read her lips. "Call Hector."

"Would you like to see the back area? We have a bar back there with a few grills," Sincere said.

Nikki hit me in my arm to distract me from the news.

"Are you okay?" Sincere asked.

"Umm, yes, I apologize. I don't need to see anymore. I'll take it." I was distraught as we sat at the bar discussing the final details as Sincere ordered us a drink.

"You ladies look like you need this."

I agreed and cracked a smile, hoping my expression didn't tell it all. We finished our drinks, and after I gave him the money, Sincere handed me a receipt, telling me he looked forward to seeing us very soon.

"Likewise," I said, getting up to leave.

I can't believe Deion! Walking out the door, I was fuming.

It was always at the forefront of my mind: Nikki was Deion's blood cousin. I could only say certain things to her. I was afraid she would tell him my thoughts in the heat of the moment. It was hard at times. I had to remain smart.

We talked for a while, mostly Nikki talking about how fine Sincere was. I wasn't feeling it, but I listened to her anyway. All the way home, I was debating if I should go to Perez myself or just call Hector. The way I looked at it, if this shit had hit the news, I wouldn't be the only one who wanted Deion dead. Perez would have to clean this mess up. He must have been tired by now if he was coming to me when Deion was not around.

We didn't know if there was a witness yet. The news did say there was one injured. *Fuck! Deion, how could you be so sloppy?* I needed to call Perez. I needed to know what he knew.

Chapter 26

I dropped Nikki off at her place. She hopped out. "Take care, Bella."

"Goodbye, Nikki. Thanks, and I'll be careful."

Driving down Transit, I made a right on Price, noticing a car turning with me. Turning again and making a left on Cottage, I checked to confirm if I was being followed. The car tailing me stayed close, and flashing lights in my rearview mirror confirmed my suspicions. I slightly pulled over to the right, and Perez pulled up beside me with his window already down.

"Follow me, Bella," he said.

"Okay," I replied, and Perez led the way.

Instead of heading toward the warehouse, he took us down by the water. I observed as he parked, scanning the area before getting out of the car. I opened my door as Perez walked toward me.

"What's going on, Perez?"

"You've probably seen the news, I assume?"

"I did. What was all that about?"

"Deion," he stated. By the looks of it, Perez's blood pressure went up as he mentioned that shit. His face turned beet red, so I knew he was mad.

I let out a giggle, smirking. "Are you mad, Perez? What do you want me to do? You're not the only one pissed at him. Lock his dumb ass up. You created this monster."

Perez looked me dead in my eyes. "If you don't help me, Bella, you will be the one in jail by morning," he said, chuckling.

"What! Are you kidding me? You already have me in this bullshit."

"I helped you with Tyrell, right?"

"I didn't need your help. And by the way, Hector was in charge of that," I said, cutting my eyes at him before placing my hand on my hip.

Perez strolled back to his car, retrieved an item, and returned with a cell phone in hand. He tapped a button, and a video started playing. As he directed it toward me, a familiar voice echoed in the air. Oh, no! Perez had captured Tyrell and me on tape.

Perez burst into laughter. "So, do I have your attention now, Miss Bella?"

"You dirty pig," I sputter. My jaw dropped as I witnessed myself striking Tyrell with the pistol.

Perez lifted his right arm as if about to strike me, making me flinch. Instead, he reached for his handkerchief, snapped it, and wiped his face.

"Hector will be reaching out to you real soon."

I swiftly retreated to my car, slamming the gas pedal and spinning my tires to escape the situation. I'd had enough of all this drama.

Back at the house, I found Deion on the couch, engrossed in some paperwork. Just looking at him made me sick to my stomach.

"What's wrong with you, Bella? Didn't you like the spot?"

"Yeah, I liked it. Did you see the news?"

"I ain't worried about that," he says, uninterested.

Mumbling under my breath, I walked into the kitchen.

"Rico will be with you for extra protection until after the party, understand?"

"Whatever." I smacked my lips, still looking out the window as Rico pulled up.

"Since you ain't worried, go open the door for Rico. Moving now is going to be hard as hell."

"What up, Bella?" Rico said.

"Hi, Rico, how are you?"

"Shit, just coolin', you know. You wanna hit this?"

"Why not? Hand it here. Dang, this is potent," I said, coughing.

Laughing, Rico said, "That's that gas, Bella. Take it easy."

"I know, right? You hungry, Rico?"

"I could eat something."

"Coo', let me see what I got." Walking in the kitchen, I looked to see what I had that was quick to cook. My stomach growled as I looked in my freezer. "Spaghetti," I yelled out to Rico.

"Yeah."

While I prepared it, I poured myself some wine in the process. Stella rosé was one of my favorites. The way it hit my taste buds was everything.

As I was marinating on the wine flavor, Deion walked up behind me and kissed me on my neck, whispering, "I love you. It smells good in here, baby."

My body tensed up as I turned to face him. "Do you love me?"

"Of course I do. Why would you ask me that?"

"I was just wondering."

I thought, *How could he be so stupid? It has to be the coke. He is not himself.*

Switching the conversation, I told him, "The Ballroom is fire. It's huge on the inside and has a VIP section with a hookah setup. They have a whole bunch of stuff going on, plus a bar outside as well."

"You hear that, nephew? Bella said the spot is fire. We about to turn up, you heard?"

Deion did the same two-step he always did. Rico started cracking up, and I did too.

We all sat down and ate dinner together, making small talk. I finished up and excused myself while they were still conversing. I was exhausted from everything that had happened earlier that day. I still couldn't believe Perez had that video. I had to get that back somehow.

As I was lying down, a text came through.

Perez: The warehouse at 24:00

I didn't respond. Another one came through. I opened it up, and a video started playing. Watching it entirely, I became furious. Immediately, I texted back.

Bella: You're a sick fuck. I can't get away.

Perez: Meet me tomorrow at the warehouse.

Bella: Deion now has Rico following me everywhere I go.

There was no reply to my last text.

I replayed the video a hundred times, watching everything that happened, making sure I didn't miss anything. I watched it so much I fell asleep to it.

I was startled out of my sleep. Deion was rubbing in between my legs while kissing my breasts, telling me how bad he wanted to fuck me.

"Stop, Deion. Stop! I'm serious." I tried to push his hands off of me. "I'm tired," I told him, slapping his hand away. He caught my arm mid-air, squeezing my wrist super tight. Grabbing my other arm, Deion put them together, pinning them both above my head with a single hand.

"That hurts, Deion. I can't move." He had me pinned beneath his body. I tried to wiggle myself away from him, but he was too strong. I started crying, panicking as he continued holding my wrists.

"Just stop, please. Deion, please."

He took his other hand and ripped off my panties as he forcefully entered me.

"Bitch, this is all I wanted," he said wickedly.

I wanted to die. At this point, all I could do was close my eyes and allow tears to fall as Deion did what he wanted to do with me, making me feel unsure of myself now as a woman.

Deion finished, and after getting off me, he smacked my leg as he turned and walked to the dresser to sniff another line of coke. I couldn't move. My mind told me to run as my body curled up in a fetal position. I just cried myself back to sleep.

Chapter 27

The next couple of weeks were stressful. Deion and I were barely on speaking terms. Rico was up my ass, and Perez was about that bullshit-ass idea. I just couldn't take it anymore. Hopefully, it would soon be all over.

I forgot I had to call mom to make sure she looked for the package I sent to her with everything I was going through.

"Mom."

"Hey, how are you?"

Clearing my throat, I told her, "I can't wait to come out there."

"You'll be here soon. By the way, I received a package you sent. It came yesterday."

"Can you please just put it up for me?"

"Yes, Bella."

"Thank you, Mom. I love you."

"I love you too, baby. Bye now."

"Bye."

Deion walked in smoothly, smiling, with one hand behind his back and the other holding a single rose.

Look at his stupid ass, I thought.

He stopped in front of me, just standing there smelling good. I watched as his left hand came from behind his back. Rolling my eyes, I saw the square black box.

"I'm sorry, Bella. I didn't mean it. It's the drugs."

Rolling my eyes, I looked at him. Deion opened the box, and my mouth slightly fell open. My eyebrows rose.

"I knew you would like it, baby."

It was an expensive diamond choker. I can't lie, it was nice. Okay, fire. But still, it didn't add up to his selfish behavior. No money or jewelry could allow me to forgive him for what he had done.

Deion took the necklace out of the box. As the box fell to the floor, he asked me to turn around, putting the choker around my neck and kissing me. His fingers grazed against my skin as he latched the clasp of the choker, laying it flat against me. The coldness from the diamonds had chills running throughout my whole body. I thanked him.

"You're welcome. Do you know what you're wearing to the party?"

"No, I don't."

"It's coming up soon. I think we should coordinate." He walked out the bedroom door.

"Whatever," I said, shrugging my shoulders.

I thought about what Perez wanted me to do. Perez had asked me to give him the route we were taking to the club. I was to text him when we were leaving The Ballroom. Perez was crazy as hell. This man had ruined my life, and now he needed me. *Ain't that about a bitch!*

Considering my circumstances, I texted him.

Bella: I will think about it.

Perez: THINK . . . there is nothing to think about.

Another text came in quickly. Looking at my phone, I frowned.

Perez: VIDEO

I was pissed as I waited to reply. Hitting the weed, I contemplated what I was going to say.

Bella: Let's make this CLEAR! I don't give a flying fuck if you tell Deion about Tyrell, but there are two conditions if you want my help.

Perez: ???

Bella: I need that phone with the video, and when our business is over with Deion, we are DONE.

Perez didn't respond. My laughter quickly turned into anger. I hated when people did that.

"I'm tired of men thinking they can just use me," I cried, hitting the blunt.

I had a whole lot of running around to do since the party was this weekend. I had to make sure everything was on schedule. It was a bittersweet moment for me. My life was about to change forever. My heart was so heavy, and my mind felt like it was about to explode from the pressure. I couldn't wait to be with my mom.

I couldn't let my emotions get the best of me right now. My kids deserved better, and so did I.

My phone started ringing. Grabbing it off the counter-top, I looked down to see it was Nikki.

"Hey, girl."

"Bella, you home? I'm about to stop by."

"Yeah."

I started rolling up so I could smoke with Nikki. As I finished, a text came in from Hector.

Hector: How are you? I have been waiting on a call or a text.

Bella: I'm good, considering.

Hector: Why didn't you call? You have been on my mind since Tyrell.

Bella: You already know what's going on. What do you want me to say?

Hector: Have dinner with me. We can discuss it then.

I took a few minutes before I texted back.

Bella: You're too kind to me. When?

Hector: I'm only here for a week. You let me know when you're free.

Nikki pulled up right on time. Getting up, I opened the door for her.

"Bella, you look like shit."

"Thanks. I miss you too."

Feeling a tug on my pants, I looked down and saw Nikki's daughter, Kiki.

"Junior? Junior?"

"Baby, he's in his room."

Kiki took off her shoes and started running fast, laughing as I watched her. She tried to get her feet to match her speed.

"I love that little girl." I felt a way to know this would be the last time we get to spend quality time together.

"What's wrong, Bella?"

Shaking my head, I replied, "Nothing. You wanna smoke?" I grabbed the blunt off the countertop.

"Yeah, we can. Girl, this party is about to be jumping. You do know that, right? I can't wait to see who all is coming."

I inhale deeply. "Yeah, it's about to be fire."

Deion entered the room, chiming in on our conversation. "Cuz, we about to turn up. You ready?"

"Hell yeah, Deion. I am so ready."

Hitting the weed, I stared at him. How could he walk around here pretending the way he did?

"That's looking real cute, Bella."

"Thank you, Nikki," I said, passing the blunt to Nikki.

"Stop acting, Bella," Deion said as he walked over, slapping my ass.

Smiling, Nikki passed the blunt back. "I have to get my hair done Friday, and I still have to find something to wear."

"I guess that gives us three days to get you right. What time is your hair appointment?"

"It's at two. Why?"

Coughing, I passed the blunt back. "Slow down. I was trying to see something. Hold on, Nikki. Let me go check on the kids real quick."

"Okay."

Peeking in, I saw the kids were good. They were playing. I heard my phone go off as I walk back into the kitchen. Grabbing it off the countertop, I look down at it. It was Perez.

Perez: Friday?

Bella: Yes

Chapter 28

Whipping up something quick, I told Nikki to roll up. As she started talking about this boutique she came across the other day, I started thinking about Perez and all this shit.

Is this shit worth it? Will I be able to live with this choice I'm about to make?

Making the plates, I heard Nikki calling my name.

"Bella, you hear me?"

"Yes, I hear you, but can you go get the kids?"

Walking out of the kitchen, Nikki went and grabbed the kids, still talking about the boutique. When she returned, she said, "Bella, they have some really cute stuff there. We should go check it out."

"Okay, sure. When should we go?"

"We can go tomorrow."

"Okay."

Watching Deion pull out of the driveway, I decided to tell Nikki what he had done. Looking over at her, my eyes started swelling as I said, "He raped me, Nikki."

She looks back at me. "Bella, what . . . what did you say?" Nikki immediately got up and walked toward me. Holding me, she started crying with me.

"I can't tell you it's going to be okay." She wiped my tears.

"This is why I got the necklace."

"I will kill him myself, Bella."

"No, I could never let you do that. The kids and I are leaving."

Stepping away from Nikki, I went upstairs to freshen up before Deion came back. Walking into the bathroom, I washed my face. Looking at myself in the mirror, I wished my life was different. Walking out, I went to my room looking for my Chapstick. As I walked over by my nightstand, I opened the blinds to let the sun in and notice an all-black Impala with tints parked outside.

Who the fuck is that? I've never seen that car on this block.

Running downstairs, I shouted to Nikki, "Look outside. Hurry."

Nikki opened the door to see the black Impala squealing away. The wheels created smoke as they took off. Shutting the door quickly, Nikki looked back over at me as she walked toward me.

"What the fuck is going on, Bella?" she said. I heard the panic in her voice. "Call Deion."

"Calm down, Nikki. Rico is on his way to the house. He was supposed to be here." To ease her mind, I texted Rico.

Bella: Rico, Wya?

I waited but got no response. Now I was calling him, and it was just ringing. I called him again.

Why the fuck is he not answering? What is going on? This is not like him at all.

"Nikki, call Deion while I try Rico again."

"Okay."

Both Nikki and I were scared. I heard it in her voice as she told Deion to come to the house. "It's an emergency."

Five minutes later, Deion pulled into the driveway. Running in the house, he yelled, "What's wrong? Y'all okay? What happened, Bella?"

"I was upstairs when I saw this black Impala with tints casing the house, just sitting there watching us."

Deion was pissed. It was all over his face as I continued telling him to look at the tire marks.

"Where the fuck is Rico?"

"I don't know." I shrugged.

Deion started yelling. "I will kill these niggas if they think they can fuck with my family." Deion searched for his phone. He pulled it from his pocket. "Has anyone spoken to Rico?"

"No, I called and texted him, but he ain't answer."

Deion started calling Rico. It just rang while on speaker phone. I watched as his veins started to pop in the middle of his forehead. Slamming down the phone, Deion paced back and forth, mumbling to himself, stroking his bald head.

Suddenly, Deion's phone went off. We all looked toward the phone.

I said a little prayer, asking it to be Rico on the other end. Thank the Lord it was. I could tell Nikki was about to say something. Her knee was bouncing as her eyebrows came together.

"Deion, what's up, cuz? What's going on witcha?" she asked.

"Fuck are you talking about?"

"You do know you have a family, right?"

"Get it off your chest, Nikki. I see you don't say shit when it's time to turn up."

Walking to the couch, Deion sat down and pulled out a baggy. Taking his keys, he dipped them into the bag. The key came back up with coke on the tip. We watched as he snorted the coke off the key, shocked.

Deion looked up at Nikki, laughing. "Why don't you worry about this party that's coming up, and I'll worry about my family over here, okay, cuz?" He laughed some more.

Nikki turned and looked at me before looking back at Deion, yelling in a high-pitch tone, "Fuck you, nigga. You will get yours." She went to get her daughter and just left.

I was so embarrassed by Deion's actions. I watched Nikki walk out the door, hurt.

"You ain't shit," I said as I stood up to go upstairs with the kids. I couldn't even look at him right now.

Walking in the boys' room, I got on the floor with Junior, and we started playing. I heard the front door open, and Deion began to talk. I listen closely for the voices.

"Where were you at?" Deion asked.

"Unc, what is the issue?"

It went silent. Then I heard my name being called.

"Yes, Deion."

"Come here for a second."

I walked down the stairs. Rico asked, "What happened, Bella? You okay?"

"Yeah, we good, Rico."

"Did you see who it was? Did you recognize what kind of car it was?"

"I don't know who it was, but it was an all-black Impala with tints."

"Unc, that sounds like that same car that was following us the other day."

"You right. I forgot about that." Jumping into action, Deion called the crew, telling them we needed more protection around the house and the best soldiers to prepare for the party. We had to tighten up security.

Hanging up, Deion started talking, looking back down at his phone. "Perez is texting me."

"What does it say, Deion?"

"He wants me to meet him in forty-five minutes."

"Well, you better get to it." I turned and walked away, knowing damn well I wanted to know what Perez wanted with him.

Rico followed me upstairs. "What up, little cousins?" He picked up Junior and started playing with him. "Bella, you wanna smoke? It's already rolled."

"Okay, that's cool. Let me get the kids right."

"I'll be downstairs."

I finished with the kids, tucking them in bed, and went back downstairs. Rico was sitting at the minibar, pouring himself a shot.

"Sorry about earlier, Bella. I should have been here."

"It's cool." I laughed, thinking how rich I would be if I had got a dollar for every time someone told me they were sorry.

Rico looked over at me. "I see you can use a drink. Here, light this, and I'll pour you one."

"Cool."

"What's up with you, Bella? You been tripping lately."

Smacking my lips, I inhaled the weed, holding it in before releasing the smoke. "Nothing, Rico. You ready for this party?"

"Ready? I been ready to fuck these bitches. Are you ready, is the question."

Laughing, I replied, "You're crazy, Rico. I will be. Don't worry about that. You got any new music you working on?"

"Yeah, a matter of fact, I just wrote some shit the other day. I gotta go lay down the track tonight."

"Spit sixteen then."

He cleared his throat, but he was interrupted when Deion came stomping through the door, slamming it behind him.

"Fuck Perez," Deion shouted.

"What just happened?"

"Change of plans. We are finding a different plug."

"Unc, you bugging."

"Deion, did you forget he is the fucking police? You can't be serious, nigga," I said.

Deion took a seat on the couch, producing that familiar little plastic bag. Emptying its contents onto the glass table, he retrieved a credit card from his wallet. Placing the card at an angle, he crushed the cocaine, creating distinct lines. Opening his wallet once more, he took out a hundred-dollar bill, rolling it into the shape of a straw. We observed as he leaned over the table, snorting a line up each nostril.

Rico and I watched in disbelief. "This is the problem, Deion," I said. "Look at you. Tell him, Rico."

"She's right, Unc. You're bugging hardbody."

"Y'all need to relax. I got this under control. Perez said he was done with us, Bella."

"What? Why?"

"I don't know. He's acting just like you bitches. That nigga can suck my dick for all I care."

Throwing my hands in the air, I got up and went upstairs to go to bed.

The following day, I noticed Deion wasn't in bed. Getting up, I went downstairs, and from the steps, I could see his feet dangling off the edge of the love seat. I noticed the disarray of beer cans around him and heard Deion's phone buzzing like crazy. Staring at him, I shook my head. He was still on the same shit from last night.

His phone went off again. Bending down slowly, I made sure he was asleep before picking up his phone. As I looked to see who it was, Deion suddenly opened his left eye, scaring me.

I dropped the phone as he said, "Did you find what you were looking for?"

"It's not like that. You need to check your shit. By the way, I have to go shopping. Can I get some money?"

Deion nodded as he answered his phone. Telling whoever was on the other end to calm down, he sat up instantly, putting on his sneakers.

"I'm on my way. Hold on right there," he said.

I was confused as I watched him scurry. "What's wrong, Deion? What's going on?"

Walking out the door, he said, "Two houses got raided." The door shut behind him.

I just stood there. Perez and Deion's meeting came to mind. "Fuck." I ran back upstairs, looking for my phone. I needed Kitty to watch the kids.

"Kitty?"

"Yes, Bella. What's going on?"

"I can't explain right now, but can you watch the kids?"

"You bringing them over?"

"Yes, I will. Thank you."

I got ready quickly, then walked into the boys' room, getting them together. Grabbing their bags, I left the house with boys.

Bella: I will be there shortly.

Nikki: Okay

Pulling up to Kitty's apartment building, I saw she was already outside, talking with her neighbor. That was right on time. I parked, getting the boys out while grabbing their bags, rushing to drop them off. I turned and ran back to the car.

I decided to drive by one of the spots, but it was already cleared. I went around the corner to hit the corner store, One Stop. Scanning the parking lot, I saw Frog.

"Frog, come here real quick."

"What's up, Bella?"

"Do you know what's up?"

"Yeah, they got raided."

"Did anybody get caught up in that?"

"You know how them niggas from the Roc be. That's who they were looking for anyways." Frog looked at me, scratching his head. "You know that wasn't the only house they hit."

"What!" Instantly, I became nauseated as I watched Frog walk away from the car. *Fuck!* Pulling out, I headed to Nikki's crib.

Getting to Nikki's, I knocked on the door a couple of times before being greeted by a familiar face grinning at me. It was Sincere.

"Well, hello, Sincere."

"What's going on, Bella? Come in."

Walking in, I went straight to the kitchen, grabbing a bottle of water. Nikki walked in.

"Am I interrupting this?" I asked.

"Girl, bye. He's about to leave." We both started laughing.

As Sincere left, he told me, "I'm looking forward to this Friday, Bella." He turned back to Nikki, kissing her. Shutting the door, she turned around, walking back into the kitchen. I just looked at her, smiling.

"When did this start, bitch? I knew it! That wasn't your first time at the club."

Shrugging, she just laughed. "Naw, it wasn't."

"Nikki, Deion lost it last night."

"What happened?"

"One word. Coke," I said, shaking my head.

"What is he thinking?"

"That is the million-dollar question. But are you ready?"

"Yes."

Chapter 29

Nikki and I shopped two days straight, savagely conquering every boutique around. Deion was going to lose it when he saw what I bought.

The morning of the party, I lay in bed for a little while before Deion walked in.

"Good morning, Bella. I was coming to wake you up. Do you have everything you need for tonight?"

"Yes. Have you been to sleep yet?" I noticed how big his eyes looked. His nose was red and runny, which put me on alert.

"Don't worry about me. Get up."

"Whatever. Give me a minute."

My phone rang as Deion walked out the door. Grabbing it, I answered.

"Hello."

"You up yet?" It was Nikki.

"Just getting up. What's going on?"

"You want to go get something to eat?"

"Shiid, why not? Deion is tripping already."

"Okay, Denny's?"

"Yeah."

Hanging up with Nikki, I jumped in the shower. The temperature was perfect up against my skin. The feeling of the waterdrops hitting my face was refreshing as I stood there, taking a moment to myself. I suddenly felt a slight chill come across my back as Deion started climbing in.

"What the fuck?"

"Can I wash your back, baby?"

"You can't be serious, Deion."

Grabbing me, he brought me closer to his body. My heart started beating super fast.

"I love you," he said. "I did all this for us. What don't you understand?"

I froze for a second. "Deion, let me go." I pulled away from him. "I never asked for this shit," I said, getting out. "I have to go meet Nikki, so I don't have time for your shit right now, Deion. Plus, you're high as fuck."

"High? You ain't seen high." He started laughing.

Turning around, I looked at him for a second before speed walking to our room to get dressed. At this point, I threw anything on that was decent. Hearing the water turn off, I put my shoes on and rushed down the steps.

"Bella! Bella," Deion called as I walked out, pretending I didn't hear him.

Getting into my car, I pulled off.

Pulling into Denny's, I parked and checked myself in the mirror before getting out. When I walked in, I saw Nikki sitting by the window.

"Hey," I said, walking up to the table.

"Bella, you okay?"

"Yeah, girl."

We chopped it up for a minute until the waitress came over to take our order.

"Nikki, I hope David and Sammy come out tonight."

"Did you call them?"

"Naw, it's too much going on."

"Well, I guess if you didn't tell them, they won't know."

"You might be right, Nikki."

Twenty minutes later, our food came. Picking over mine, I wasn't really hungry. I couldn't stop thinking about tonight. Time was flying by, and nervousness started to creep in. Standing up, I walked to the counter to pay for our food. Looking back at Nikki, it dawned on me. This was the last breakfast we would have together.

Leaving, we stood by our cars, talking a little bit longer.

"Bella, are we pregaming?"

"We can."

"What time you want me to come over?"

"I don't care. Come whenever."

Silence came between us as Nikki realized this would be the last time we did this. She walked closer to me. Her eyes were watery as she embraced me with all she had. I hugged her back.

"It's going to be okay. I won't be gone forever," I tell her.

Letting me go, Nikki looked at me as she wiped her face. "You better not, Bella."

Getting in our cars, we drove off, heading in different directions. This shit hurt. It was not fair. "I fucking hate you, Deion," I screamed from the top of my lungs, hitting the dashboard. I convinced myself I was doing this for all the right reasons.

Buzz, buzz, buzz.

I pulled over to find my phone in my purse. It was Perez.

Perez: We good for tonight?

Bella: Yessss

Perez: Address

Bella: 724 Main Street

Driving around the block a couple of times, I tried to pull it together. Turning down Washington Street, the next block over from the house, I saw the same black Impala with tints. It caught my attention, of course. I pulled over on the side of the road behind this white F150 Ford pickup truck, hoping they couldn't see me. I just had to see who this was.

I wasn't even there ten minutes, and guess who pulled up? Perez. Fuck!

What in the hell is going on? Shit!

It was Rico! I felt my forehead crease as my eyes widened. I stared so hard as panic set in.

"What the fuck?" I didn't even want to know what Perez had on him.

As Rico walked back to his car, I scooched down in my seat, watching Perez pull off in my direction. He slowed down and our eyes met. I was scared as hell, but he kept going.

Rico pulled off, and so did I. By the time I hit the corner, he was already at the house.

Walking in the house, I just glared at him out of the corner of my eye, still in shock about what I had just seen.

"What up, Bella," Rico said.

"Shit," I said, walking straight past him, going upstairs.

There was a knock at the bedroom door.

"Who is it?"

The door opened, and Deion walked in. "What time you getting ready?"

"I don't know yet."

"What time do you want to leave?"

"Ughhh, I don't know. Fuck."

"You need to check the attitude," he said, walking back out the door.

I lay on the bed for a while, finishing the blunt I had. Shit was out of control. Closing my eyes, I prayed to God, hoping He was watching over my boys and me.

As day turned into night, I got up and collected my things before going into the bathroom. I decided I wanted a glass of wine, so I went downstairs. I overheard Deion talking with Rico. I tried listening, but they were speaking so low.

"Rico, something is not right. I can feel it, nephew."

"Unc, you tripping. We are good. We got goons on deck, you heard!"

Making my presence known, I called out, "What's up, y'all? You guys ready for tonight?"

Deion stared at me without speaking, deep in thought. "Yeah, we about to get it in, Bella."

Pouring my wine, I went back toward the living room when Deion stopped me. Smiling, I walked into the kitchen. Looking out the window, I saw a couple of niggas standing outside, talking. Shaking my head, I wondered who wee they supposed to protect.

"What's up? Nikki should be here in a few," I said. They both looked at me crazy. "What? She is family. Or did y'all forget?"

"A'ight, Bella. Rico will be driving with you tonight."

"Naw, I'm good. I can drive myself. Plus we're picking up Nikki's homegirl."

Deion looked at me, knowing I was lying.

"Word. It's like that, Bella?" Rico said.

"It's nothing personal, Rico. Don't take it that way." Turning around, I walked upstairs, grumbling. "Niggas think they're so slick."

When I reached the top of the steps, I heard my phone go off. Walking into the room, I set my wine down and grabbed my phone.

Perez: I saw you.

Bella: Okay, and I saw you.

Perez: Remember the deal. Your freedom for his life.

I didn't text back.

Sipping on my wine, I thought, *It's almost over*. Lighting up the blunt, I pondered at the same time, asking God why. I promised Him if He saw me through this, I would change my life.

My phone rang, startling me. It was Mom.

"Hello, Mom."

"What you doing, baby?"

"Not too much. About to get ready for this party. Whatcha doing?"

"I was thinking about you. Are you okay?"

"Yeah, Mom, we're coming. Don't be surprised if I knock on your front door." I let out a slight giggle and told her I had to go.

"I love you, baby."

Finishing my glass of wine, I got up and started running my bathwater. I turn on 93.7 WBLK, setting the mood. They were about to cut up since it was Friday, dropping heat back-to-back. I sat on the side of the tub, taking a couple of pulls of a cigarette, thinking about how Rico believed he was so slick.

"Bella. Bella."

"What?" I yelled back. I knew damn well that was not Nikki screaming my name like that.

I heard her walking up the steps, then the door opened.

"Girl, hurry up."

"Nikki, give me a minute to wash up, and I'll be out."

"Okay." She looked in the mirror, checking her makeup. Nikki turned around, telling me again to hurry up as she closed the door to go back downstairs.

I washed up quickly and jumped out. Already knowing what I was about to wear made it that much more convenient. Grabbing the lotion, I walked into the room. Dropping my towel, I made sure my body was nice and soft. The lotion had a nice shimmer, giving me a beautiful glow. I looked over at the bed. My dress was laid perfectly across it with my all-white Christian Louboutin.

"Girl, what are you doing?"

"Getting ready, Nikki." I hated the feeling of being rushed. Honestly, I didn't even want to go. I couldn't even enjoy myself knowing someone wouldn't make it home.

Leaving the room, I told myself that no matter what happened tonight, it was about the kids.

Walking down the steps slowly, I held onto the railing, making sure I didn't miss a step. Stopping abruptly on the last one, I caught everyone's attention. Deion looked at me in amazement, his mouth slightly open as he started rubbing his hands together.

"Wow, baby, you fine."

"Thank you."

"Bella, you look beautiful. Looking like you just stepped out of a *Vogue* magazine."

"Thank you, Rico."

"The whole family is on point, especially you, Nikki. Spin around let me get a good look at what you're wearing," I said.

Nikki had on a short, all-white fitted mini dress, strapless, with white-and-black snakeskin heels and a matching bag. She had her hair pinned up with a cute clip on the side. It brought out her chocolate skin tone that glowed so perfectly.

"Wow, you look beautiful, cuz!"

"Thank you."

"Sincere is very lucky to have found you," I said, smiling.

Deion and Rico interrupted us, of course, hollering "Flicks."

We took some pictures by our bar and then next to the fireplace. I took some of just Deion and Rico, and they snapped some of me and Nikki.

Deion pulled me to the side. "Make sure you stay close behind us."

"Okay."

Going outside, we got in two separate vehicles. Nikki and I jumped in my car, while Deion, Rico, and a few other people jumped in his truck.

***

Making a stop, Deion pulled into One Stop. He got out and walked over to me.

"Do you need anything out of here?" he asked.

"Yeah, grab me something to drink and a blunt."

Nodding, he walked in. Coming back out shortly, he handed me my stuff. "Make sure you stay right behind me."

"Okay, Deion. I told you I would."

"Just listen for once, Bella. Fuck!"

Deion jumped back in his truck, and I followed as we hit I-90.

"Here, roll this up, Nikki."

"A'ight."

I took a swig of the bottle as I listened to the radio, trying to get hyped. I was on edge, even though my demeanor was good on the outside. It was my inside that was fucked up, not knowing how the night would unfold.

Hopping off on our exit, I was still behind Deion. We hit a few side streets before pulling up to the club.

"Bitcchhh, look at all these people out here," Nikki yelled.

"Nikki, they are wrapped around the block."

I watched Rico as he pulled in front of The Ballroom, throwing the truck in park. Deion stepped out, and immediately everybody stared at him like he was somebody. Walking toward me, he came up and opened my door.

"You ready, love?"

"Yes, Deion."

Getting out of the car, the feeling was surreal. We felt like hood celebrities as we walked in. The DJ was spinning all the new joints. As we walked past the bar, the DJ shouted out Deion's name. I watched him raise his arm, saluting the crowd. This was a proud moment for him. The red-and-blue lights highlighted his movements as he walked toward the VIP section, holding my hand.

Chapter 30

"Yo, Unc, this shit is off the hook!" exclaimed someone in the crowd.

"What did you expect?" Deion responded, a smile playing on his lips. "Bella did her thing. Now, pass that bottle, Rico. We trying to start this party. Whoo!"

The atmosphere was electric. The dance floor was packed, and Kat, behind the oval-shaped bar, worked tirelessly to keep the drinks flowing.

"This shit's crazy. Sincere made sure we were good. I want this moment to last forever," I remarked, a smile gracing my face. Everyone had shown up and showed out for Deion, and the night was in full swing.

Amidst the celebration, a dispute arose at the bar, catching Sincere's attention. He swiftly handled the situation before joining us.

"I just handled that at the bar. Y'all good?" he inquired.

"Yeah, we good," Deion confirmed.

Leaning over, Deion whispered in my ear, "You ready?"

"Yes."

As we stood up, gunshots started spraying throughout the club. *Rat-a-tat! Bratat! Rat-a-tat bratat!* I started screaming, and so did Nikki. Deion pulled his gun from his waist, putting one in the chamber as he yanked me down by my arm.

"Stay low and keep up," he said.

"Okay," I yelled, looking around us as we moved through the chaos.

Everybody was scattering, running around, scream-ing, trying to take shelter. Continuing to follow closely, Sincere maneuvered us to his office. Letting us out of his private entrance was a good look.

"Thank you, Sincere," I said while Deion dapped him up.

"If you need anything, get a hold of me. I gotcha," Sincere said, walking over to Nikki. "All right, y'all be safe out there. I'll call you later, Nikki," he said, leaning in and kissing her cheek.

We started walking down this disgustingly long, filthy alleyway. It smelled like piss and shit. Cardboard boxes were lined up against the fence to the left of Rico, near some dumpsters. Trash was falling out everywhere. Soiled diapers and fast-food wrappers filled big-ass potholes that were in the street. As we got closer to the end, I heard a lot of commotion. Gunshots still echoed between the buildings, making my adrenaline pump. The smell of gunpowder made me gasp.

Deion looked at me, gripping my hand tighter as we turned the corner. Folks were running around, scream-ing as they got into their cars. Panic rose inside me, and my palms became clammy as Deion got us in the car. I watched as he got in his truck safely.

"Bella, what the fuck happened?"

"I don't know, Nikki. Maybe it had something to do with that little dispute at the bar. Go ahead and call Sincere."

I glanced over across the street, and a fresh candy apple red Hummer caught my attention. It was sitting pretty. I nudge Nikki's elbow to get her attention.

"Look at that Hummer," I told her.

"Bella, what? You see I'm on the phone."

"Oops, I forgot," I whispered.

Deion pulled off, jumping in traffic, and I followed behind him, trying to keep up. I watched closely as Deion maneuvered through the streets. Taking a quick left then a right, he made it through the yellow light, but I didn't.

"Fuck!" I pounded my steering wheel in frustration.

"Shit," I mumbled, trying not to panic. Catching the vehicle out of my peripheral view, I wondered why they were creeping. Keeping it cool, I turned my head slowly, watching in disbelief as the back window started coming down. A smoke cloud flowed out, along with a red dot pointing in my direction. I froze before stepping on the gas. They cut me off, making me swerve as they jumped on the thruway.

"Fuck you assholes," I screamed, making sure they could hear me.

My phone started vibrating.

"Who is it?" Nikki asked.

"Perez. Open it up. Read it to me."

"Okay. . . . It's just question marks."

Shaking my head, I told her not to respond.

Seeing lights in the distance fucked up my train of thought, capturing my attention quickly. "Nikki, you see that?"

"Yeah, get closer. I can't tell what it is."

"Bitch, are they disappearing? Oh, shit!" My forehead wrinkled as I raised my eyebrows, watching Deion's truck flip multiple times. I tried to speed up. "What the fuck! Nikki, call nine one one," I screamed at the top of my lungs. I started hyperventilating.

Looking over at Nikki, she was stuck with her mouth open. I screamed Nikki's name. She snapped back and called 911.

"Yes, we are on I-Ninety driving eastbound, and my cousin, he—"

Putting the car in park, I took off running, screaming Deion's name, hoping he would call mine back. As I got closer to the truck, I noticed body parts on the ground covered with blood, along with scattered clothing. Rico's sneakers solidified it for me.

"Fuck, fuck! No, no, nooo," I said, shaking my head, turning slowly toward the truck. Fear rushed through my body as I stared at all those bullet holes. I crouched over and fell to my knees. Weak and trying to regulate my breathing, I heard a faint noise causing me to move cautiously around the vehicle as the noise faded. Opening the driver's side of the door, I saw Deion struggling to breathe. Reaching around him, I undid his seatbelt.

"You better not leave me now, Deion."

He was coughing out blood. I watched as it slid down his chin. "I'm sorry . . ." He coughed. "I lovvv . . ."

"Deion. Deion . . . no . . . no, baby, wake up."

I watched as Deion took his last breath. Hitting him in the chest, I screamed hysterically. "No, nooo, God! Nooooo." I heard sirens faintly in the background.

Nikki walked over to me, trying to pull me away from Deion. "He's gone, Bella. Get up. There's nothing you can do."

"I can't leave him, Nikki. Not like this. I just can't."

The paramedics rushed over toward me, helping Nikki to pick me up.

"Get the fuck off of me and go check on Deion," I spat, collapsing to the ground.

Turning around quickly, they went to the truck. From the looks on their faces, I could tell he was dead.

A state trooper picked me up off the ground and escorted me away from the truck.

"What happened here?" he asked.

I couldn't stop crying to answer him. He walked over to Nikki, asking her.

"Do you know what happened here, ma'am?"

"We saw something that looked like fireworks, a lot of flashing lights. They appeared out of nowhere. Then they disappeared. Bella tried to get closer to see, but the only thing we saw was Deion's truck flipping over multiple times on the highway."

The officer looked at me. "Were you the first to arrive?"

No words would come out as I nodded my reply.

"Bella, here. Your phone is vibrating," Nikki said, handing it to me.

I grabbed it from her and glanced at it. Perez. *You fuckin' gotta be kidding me.*

Perez: I will see you later.

Not responding, I kept my attention on the paramedics as they brought up each of the bodies in separate black bags, one by one. Crying in disbelief, Nikki tried to comfort me. I looked up at the state trooper. He was staring at us weirdly. I will never forget this.

Turning his head sharply, he saw the news people approaching the scene. He handed me his card and told me, "Miss Goins, by the way, Hector sends his regards."

In a dead stare, I tilted my head. "Huh? Qhat the fuck did you just say?"

"Bella, we gotta go. Come on," Nikki said.

Running back to the car, I was a mess, still agitated by what had just happened. Jumping in, we pulled off.

Somehow, I managed to get us home safe. Walking up to the door, I noticed it was ajar. I looked behind me nervously, making sure Nikki was right there. We eased our way inside.

I turned on the living room lights first, grabbing my bat from behind the couch. Tiptoeing toward the kitchen, I tried not to make any noise. Turning on the lights, I looked around cautiously, checking my shit. In the center of my kitchen table, I saw a cell phone, along with a note.

"What does it say, Bella?"

"It says to throw out my phone and keep this one. Love, Hector."

"Bella, who is Hector?"

Slipping the phone in my bra, I quickly went upstairs to pack a light bag for me and the kids. Nikki was on guard, looking out for anything that didn't look right. I still had to call Kitty to let her know I was coming. I practiced my breathing along with my tone out loud, making sure I didn't mess it up.

My bra started ringing, making me jump. I pulled it out and opened up the text message. A video started playing. I watched Perez in a cooler, butt-ass naked, hanging from a metal trolley rail. Beaten, his bloody and bruised body was limp. I could tell he was on the brink of death. Suddenly, one of Hector's men walked in front of the camera, holding a sign.

In big letters, it read: NEVER BITE THE HAND THAT FEEDS YOU.

Closing out the message, I called Kitty.

"Hello, Kitty."

"Bella, what time is it? Why are you calling so late?"

"I need to come to get the boys. It's an emergency."

"What? What happened, Bella?"

"I can't explain. Please, just get the kids ready."

"Okay, come on over."

"Thank you, Kitty."

Leaving the house shortly after that, I still needed to drop Nikki off. On my way to her house, my bra went off again, startling me and causing me to swerve. As I reached for it, another text message came in.

"Who is that, Bella?"

"I don't know, and I don't want to know."

I couldn't respond right now. Pulling up in front of Nikki's apartment before she stepped out, I told her, "Take care, friend." I cracked half a smile.

Reaching around, she hugged me. "Call me when you get settled," she sobbed.

"Okay." Driving off, I pulled over up the street to open the text.